Happy Ghoulidays II

Happy Ghoulidays II

Shannon Lawrence

Warrior Muse Press

Table of Contents

One for Sorrow

Bridget tucked her coat tighter against the cold Chicago wind. To her right, the waters of the river shone green in the sparse sunlight breaking through the clouds. Revelers in a neaby pub hollered words to various songs in drunken voices, despite it only being noon. Some people had grabbed an early start for the green beer drinking.

It was tempting to grab a beer with everyone else, since her boss had let her out of work early. Her and everyone. He'd sung out, "Go and be Irish!" which felt questionable to her in terms of being appropriate, but she really was Irish ancestrally and she couldn't work up the energy being offended would take. Also, they never should have been at work on a Saturday, anyway. Now *that* was offensive. Still, they'd gone in expecting to have a full workday, so it was a pleasant surprise, albeit one that should never have been an issue. The fact that she felt any gratitude for the "early" release was telling, and something she'd need to revisit later.

Chicago always went all out for St. Patrick's Day, and this year was no different. It seemed like half the people passing her wore some sort of green. She'd made a token effort by putting a green bow in her hair, which was really more about keeping away any pinchers who thought they were clever. As far as Bridget was aware, there was nothing in Irish history that made pinching someone not wearing green a thing, which meant it was just some stupid act Americans had come up with. It seemed more like an excuse to be a dick.

Bridget's brisk walk took about twenty minutes. When she arrived at her apartment building, the ripe smell of death greeted her. Peering over at the road, she noticed a magpie pecking at a flattened snake that had clearly been run over. The gorgeous blue, black, and white bird's sharp beak quickly severed the snake's head from the rest of the body. The bird picked up the head in its beak, glanced at Bridget, then flew away, leaving the bedraggled, headless corpse behind.

Bridget shuddered and went inside.

As the elevator rose to her floor, the first line of an old nursery rhyme about magpies her nana used to tell her drifted through her mind: *One for sorrow.*

She'd never really paid it much attention, but now she tried to remember the rest of the words. Had it meant that seeing just one magpie would lead to sorrow? The last thing she needed right now was for something bad to happen. Given, that was true at any moment, but right now she was in a happily committed relationship, on the verge of a promotion at work, and generally happy with the way things were.

Thinking of her relationship reminded Bridget that she needed to call Gene about going out tonight. She'd thought it wouldn't be until late, but now that she had the whole day before her, they could plan a nice dinner out before hitting a pub. It wasn't actually St. Patrick's Day yet, but the city liked to celebrate it on the weekend and then again on the actual day.

Speaking of revelry, the gaudy sounds of the parade a few blocks away penetrated the windows. Brass instruments and drums, cheers, and voices over loudspeakers were a background hum of unpleasant proportions. Bridget decided to take a hot bath first before calling Gene. There was plenty of time, and a bath sounded especially pampering and self-indulgent. She could listen to some music or a podcast to block out the sounds coming from the street and relax.

She quickly gathered items that appealed to her, including a snack of cut up apples and peanut butter, a glass of iced tea, and a frozen eye mask. It had been months at least since she'd had a Saturday to herself. As the hot water poured into the tub, steaming up the window next to it, Bridget tied her hair up into a sloppy bun to keep it out of the water. Then she climbed in, hissing a breath through her teeth at the feel of the nearly scalding water. Her skin instantly turned red, and she slid the rest of the way in, delighting in the feel of it. The liquid heat enveloped her. Lying back, she started some music and put the ice mask over her eyes.

Two for joy was the next line in the nursery rhyme. Now she remembered that much. It just popped into her head. With that, the next two lines came, thanks to the rhyme: *three for a girl, four for a boy.* Not something she had to worry about any time soon. But now the next lines wouldn't come, and her attention returned to the music, a tiny beat of concern still in the back of her mind about the single magpie and its possible omen. It was hard to overcome childhood teachings, no matter how absurd.

Her thoughts drifted to Gene. He wasn't who she had envisioned being with, yet their relationship worked. He was her perfect foil. They weren't the same person, more like two sides of the same coin. Opposites, really, but with the same goals. He was kind and patient, gentle, an optimist. She was often impatient and boisterous, planning for the things that might go wrong. Yet his support of her made it easier to live in the moment.

Her body hummed with pleasure as she thought about Gene. She finished the bath and curled up in bed for a nap. The weight and heat of her comforter helped sleep come quickly.

***

Evening had gathered as Bridget slept, and she awoke to a dark room. Shadows snaked across the wall as an ambulance screeched by on the street, its lights blasting through her window. She snatched up her cell phone to check the time and saw that she'd missed a text. It had come in about twenty minutes earlier, at 6:48 PM: *Still on for O'Leary's @ 8?* So much for dinner ahead of time, but she'd obviously needed the sleep and O'Leary's had good Irish pub fare.

She sent a quick text: *C U there.*

Jumping out of bed, Bridget got dressed, put on her makeup, pulled her hair up into some semblance of "style," and raced out the door, pulling on her coat on the way to the elevator. O'Leary's wasn't far, and despite the heavy traffic out, she made it there on foot, walking in at 8:02. She allowed a celebratory internal whoop and searched through the sea of bodies for Gene's bearded face. Someone bumped her from behind, and she stumbled forward, knocking into a man in front of her. He smiled and grasped her arms to settle her, then turned back to his friends.

Bridget worked her way through the crowd, having to brush past the copious bodies. Everything and everyone reeked of beer. Voices swirled in a cacophony of drunken shouting, everyone trying to be heard over everyone else. Faces surrounded her, mouths agape. She started to sweat, not finding Gene anywhere. It felt like she'd been around the entire bar with no luck. Her breaths came quicker. Her chest got tight. The crowd jostled her. There were too many people.

She turned back toward the door and tried to make her way out, pushing now at those in front of her, bumping them with her shoulder, anything to move them out of her way. Panic overtook her, heart pounding. Tunnel vision developed.

Then a strong, warm hand grasped her upper arm.

Bridget reacted without thinking, thoroughly in the throes of a panic attack. She grabbed the hand and squeezed, turning at the same time. She brought up her imprisoned arm, her hand landing on his chest to shove him away.

She looked up into Gene's face, and relief instantly swept through her. Throwing her arms around him, she buried her face in his warm neck. His beard scratched at her face, but she didn't care. He wrapped his arms around her in return, and the warmth of his body helped calm her heart, breaths returning to normal.

Gene gently led her to a high table along the side wall and helped her get seated. He yelled over the surrounding voices, "You okay?" His eyes crinkled in concern.

Bridget nodded, plastering on a smile. She was used to crowds. Living in downtown Chicago guaranteed it. Why she'd had a panic attack, she didn't know, but it was done now and she wanted to have fun. Panic attacks rarely made sense in the first place. Her pulse slowed, the ache in her chest easing.

Gene pushed a drink across the table. He'd already gotten

her a glass of wine. He sipped his own green beer, foam decorating his mustache until he wiped it away. "I ordered us burgers."

She took a sip of her wine and let the rich, fruity flavor roll over her tongue. A couple swallows later, and the alcohol seeped through her muscles, letting them melt. She forgot the panic and focused on enjoying the evening and chasing the buzz. Another glass of wine later, the food arrived.

The rest of the evening was a blur of bars, drinking, and dancing. They headed to her apartment sometime after midnight, caught up in the lessening crowds of the street as they made their way through the chilly air and across the cold concrete. In the elevator, Gene pressed her back against the wall and lifted her until she wrapped her legs around his waist. They kissed passionately, tongues dancing. She tightened her legs, feeling the solid press of his excitement against her.

His mouth released hers and he ran his tongue down the sensitive skin of her neck. As he made his way down her chest, the doors opened behind him.

Bridget moaned, not ready to stop.

They moved off the elevator to her front door, where he kissed the back of her neck and shoulder while she tried to unlock it. His hands slid around to the front, grasped her breasts. Frantic to get inside, she missed the slot repeatedly until the key finally slid into place.

Inside the door, she dropped her coat and kicked off her shoes. She grabbed his shirt and pulled him toward her.

Gene shut the door and undid her buttons, one by one, until her chest was bared to his wandering hands and mouth.

Somehow they got to the bedroom, and he roughly threw her back onto the bed. In one fluid movement, he removed her dress.

Bridget, head swimming with wine, worked at the button of his jeans. She got the zipper down and shoved his pants back. He pulled his shirt off over his head and tossed it, then stepped out of his pants.

He was on her, inside her, everywhere at once.

Everything spun, and she had a moment to think she'd drunk too much, that she felt sick. She didn't want him to stop,

5

though, so she kept going, squeezing her legs around his waist to pull him closer.

She opened her eyes, and the face above hers wasn't Gene's. There was no beard, and his hair was red and straight instead of Gene's dark curls. His eyes were bright blue, unlike Gene's brown ones. Bridget tried to push him away. "Wait. Stop."

He didn't stop.

The man thrust harder, deeper. He grabbed her throat and squeezed. He grinned down at her, slamming himself into her.

She tried to scream, but couldn't make a sound against the pressure of his hands.

She scratched at him, trying to get his eyes, but he shook off the blows and scratches. Even when blood trickled down his face, he kept squeezing and thrusting.

He was hurting her. Too deep, his thrusts pounded painfully inside her. Her lungs burned. The tendons in her throat strained.

Everything grew blurry. His features kept changing. Feathers sprouted from his face. His eyes turned beady and black. His nose lengthened into a cold, hard beak.

One for sorrow, thought Bridget.

She passed out.

***

Bridget awakened to the glare of sunlight and Gene asleep next to her. He looked peaceful, serene.

Dread filled her at the sight of him. She climbed out of bed, body tense, trying to be as quiet as possible so she wouldn't wake him. A sharp pain in her pelvis drew a hiss. She went into the bathroom and locked the door. Blood stood out starkly on her inner thighs. Her throat ached. Looking in the mirror, she saw bruising where his fingers had squeezed. He'd never done anything like that before. Never even been rough. He was a gentle lover. Something had gotten into him.

The memory of the feathers came back, and she fought against the fuzziness in her brain to figure out what had actually happened last night. She remembered scratching him, but his face was unmarked. And what of the red-haired stranger she'd seen? Clearly, the beak and feathers couldn't have been real. Had Gene looked different before or after his hands had closed around her throat?

She sat down on the toilet and winced at the searing pain urinating caused. Closing her eyes, she forced herself to relax and finish. It burned even after she was done.

Something moved in her abdomen. A lazy roll. She placed a hand under her navel, but jerked it away when she felt the same roll from the outside.

There was something inside her.

Bridget fought against the building panic. There couldn't be anything inside her. It was something weird with her intestines, was all.

The roll came again. This time she didn't touch it.

Double checking that the door was locked, she stepped into the shower, turned the water on as hot as it would go, and crouched on the ground, letting the droplets pound on her back. She wrapped her arms around her legs and tucked her chin between her knees. Blood swirled down the drain. Bile burned up the back of her throat, the acidic taste coating her tongue. She closed her eyes. Water ran down her face, her back, everywhere, and soothed the oncoming panic attack.

He was still out there.

They'd been dating for two years, and nothing like this had ever happened. There had been no indications that he even had a single violent bone in his body. Her entire body quaked and tears burned her eyes.

A knock sounded at the bathroom door.

Bridget's entire body tensed. She stared at the door, willing it to stay closed.

The doorknob turned.

He knocked again.

"Bridge?"

She opened her mouth. Closed it again.

"I have to head out. I'll give you a call later."

She held her breath.

***

Bridget didn't know how long she'd stayed in the shower, waiting, afraid to leave. The water had gone cold, chasing her out. Even then, she'd stayed in the bathroom, heart pounding, alert to any noise that might tell her he was still out there. The shower had covered any possible sound of departure.

Finally, she'd strayed out, put on warm clothes, and climbed back into the bed. Eventually, she fell asleep, awakened by her phone ringing. She didn't check the caller ID, just rolled over and went back to sleep.

When she was awake, she felt movement inside her abdomen. It seemed to be growing. At one point, she curled her legs into the fetal position, but she couldn't handle feeling the sensation of movement on both the inside and against her thighs, so she stretched her legs out and slept on her back.

It was dark the next time she woke up. Her phone showed a message and multiple texts. She didn't want to talk to him, didn't want to think about him. Her memories of that morning were sharp. She kept expecting them to fade or to straighten out into some semblance of normalcy, but they replayed exactly the same way every time. She considered what she could have done differently, but he'd been strong, so strong, his hands sealing off her windpipe. His body had held her down.

That mattered less than what grew inside her now. She knew it was physically impossible to be pregnant. Intellectually, she knew there couldn't be anything inside her. That didn't change what she felt. Or what she finally saw when she grew brave enough.

Lying on her back, Bridget pulled back the blankets and lifted her shirt. Her abdomen bulged in two different places, the skin pulled so tight it looked shiny.

She reached out a shaking, tentative hand and touched one of the bulges.

They both moved simultaneously. Coiling.

A sob escaped Bridget's throat.

She yanked the blankets up, rolled onto her side, and willed herself to fall asleep. No longer caring what she felt, she pulled her knees in tight and tucked her hands to her throat. All she wanted was the dark release of sleep. Instead, she watched her encounter with Gene play in her head repeatedly, starkly, in full detail. She saw the face again, tried to place it. Couldn't. Her mind worked on a loop all night.

When the sun came up, wounding her already scratchy eyes, Bridget picked up her phone, saw more texts, didn't care. She never had to speak to him again. He would get the hint sometime.

Then she sat up, panic once more making her heart pump. He had a key. Gene had a key to her apartment. If she didn't respond, he might show up. She picked up her phone and texted *Stomach bug. Will call you when I feel better.*

She didn't want to read anything he'd written. Nor did she want to listen to his message. When he responded, she looked at the preview on her phone's screen, saw it said, *ok*, and figured that had bought her some time.

The thing in her abdomen was bigger. Her stomach rumbled, and the thing moved again. Now there were three lumps, thicker than before.

Bridget looked up her doctor's number and called, hoping they were open.

"Hello?"

"Yes, hi, I need to see Dr. Longan. Today, if possible."

"Is this an emergency?"

She looked at her belly, at what looked like coiled ropes inside her body. "Yes."

"We don't have any appointments today. If it's an emergency, you should go to the emergency room."

Bridget couldn't respond. Tears choked her throat. She hung up.

The thought of climbing out of bed was terrifying. Her midriff felt heavy. She didn't want to feel it shift. She wanted to stay still like a mouse and wait for it to pass. Her stomach rumbled again, and she realized she hadn't eaten since yesterday. How could she feel so empty and so full at the same time?

As slowly as she could, Bridget moved the covers and eased to the side of the bed. She sat up first, dangling her feet off the side. Dizziness roiled through her head, and tunnel vision formed, everything greying around the edges. She put her head down toward her knees, surprised to find she couldn't bend as far as usual. Her abdomen blocked it. The swollen flesh lay heavy on her lap, skin pink and shining. Part of her knew a woman's uterus and skin could stretch much farther than this, but she still feared her flesh would tear and spill whatever this was out on the floor.

Disturbed, it rolled once more, the bulges in her belly shifting. Something that looked like a snout poked at her skin, smaller than the other bulges, sharper. It grazed across her abdomen before disappearing.

Bridget pushed her shirt down, steeled herself, and stood up. The weight in her belly made her feel sluggish. She was weak. Moving carefully, she went to the kitchen to grab some food. It would take energy to make anything real, but there were leftovers from Chinese takeout the other day. She opened the top and dug in with a fork, but the moment she put the cold noodles in her mouth, she grew queasy and gagged. The roll of the noodles against her tongue were too similar to the feel of the thing inside her. She spit them back out into the white package and chucked it in the garbage can.

Roving through the fridge, she found cheese and bread, and slapped together a couple sandwiches. Then she ate an apple and some carrot sticks. The more she ate, the more the creature moved, but also the hungrier she got. Her abdomen boiled with movement. She dragged an ice cream tub out of the freezer and discovered it was three-quarters full. She ate it with a fork directly from the tub, surprised to discover that it was much easier than eating hard ice cream with a spoon.

Her phone rang in the bedroom, and she realized she was missing work. No way she'd be going in like this. She knew she should go to the doctor, but she didn't know what to say, so she climbed back into bed and slept again, stomach and uterus both full.

***

The next couple days passed in a haze of sleeping and eating. The creature grew, and now she was certain that it was a snout pressing against her abdomen sometimes. Something had gone numb in her mind. She knew she should be scared, that she should be seeking help, but she was so tired and hungry, and the thought of going out into the cold made her more so. She wanted to nest down in her blankets, despite the wrappers and packages burying the covers. Her stomach was huge, and she had to walk with her hands supporting her belly, feeling that at any moment she would topple over or split open. But no, the stomach stretched and grew, and the creature got bigger and bigger, its weight a constant ache.

Somewhere in the fog, there was pounding on the door. Gene's voice called her name. "Go away!" she thought she screamed. "I never want to talk to you again." She remembered whimpering, "You hurt me." Then it was back into the haze.

When she woke up on the kitchen floor, covered in crumbs, vomit, and food stains, it awakened something in her. The numbness pulled back, and she looked at herself as she should have been for days. She could barely move. Breathing had become hard. Eating gave her acid reflux. Her organs were being shoved higher each day, compacted like garbage in a truck.

She barely made it into her bedroom to grab her cellphone, where she dialed 9-1-1.

"You've reached 9-1-1. Who am I speaking with?" The operator sounded calm, professional.

"Bridget."

"What's your emergency?"

Bridget struggled to talk. "S-s-something's...wrong with m-me."

"Have you been injured, Bridget?"

"I guess so."

"What's the nature of your injury?"

"Something is inside me."

Keys clacked on the other end of the line. "Were you stabbed? Shot?"

"No. I don't know what's wrong. I c-can't move."

"What's your address? I'll send an ambulance out."

Bridget gave her address. "I need to get the chain off the door."

"Can you do so safely?"

"I-I think so."

"Okay. I need you to remain on the phone. Are you able to take it with you?"

"Yes."

Bridget got up from the bed and moved toward the front door. Her belly strained so much that it hurt. The thing inside her moved as if it were stretching, the coils widening, pressing outward and upward. She wheezed against the pressure on her lungs.

About halfway to the door, the movements increased in intensity. Instead of the minor shifts that had been occurring over the last few days, it now appeared to be changing positions entirely. The changing positions were visible through the cotton of her shirt, bumps appearing and disappearing, flesh stretching and rolling.

She pushed on to the front door, where she pulled the chain, unlocked the door, and opened it before slumping to the floor.

The movements didn't stop.

Frantic, Bridget, pulled her shirt up to see what was happening. The shape she had identified as a head and snout appeared, pushing against the flesh of her belly and moving downward. It disappeared again, other bumps taking its place.

The faint voice of the dispatcher called out of the phone, which still rested in her hand where it had settled on the ground. "Ma'am? Bridget? Are you still there?"

Bridget panted against the sensations playing out in her body. She dropped the phone and pressed both hands to her pelvis, where sharp pain tore at her.

"Oh my God," she said. "I think it's trying to get out."

When several people in blue uniforms walked through her door, Bridget screamed, "Get it out of me! Get it out!" She couldn't stop. There was so much pressure.

A man leaned down to put his face in her sight. "Are you pregnant, Bridget?"

"No," she panted. "Get it out."

Their voices were noise, a jumble. She couldn't tell what they were saying. There were hands on her. Pressure everywhere. Once more she found herself surrounded by too many people, too many voices. She couldn't breathe.

Then she was moving, a hard surface beneath her, something tying her down.

Looking up, she saw only faces, the ceiling, walls, more faces.

Their voices kept going. She couldn't tell if they were talking to her.

It didn't matter.

She could feel the coils moving, something slithering down, down, down.

Bridget screamed. No words. Just shrieks, more noise.

She was in the ambulance, then at the hospital. The misery was never ending. The pressure shifted down. She could feel it trying to force its way out.

A face appeared over her, and she tried to focus. He had red hair, pulled back into a ponytail. There were scratches on his face.

"Hello, I'm Dr. Kelly, but you can call me Patrick." His face was kind, his voice calm.

Bridget tried harder to focus against the pain and terror.

"Lucky you, you got an Irishman on St. Patrick's Day."

Lucky?

He wore green scrubs. On his arm, she saw a tattoo of magpies. Seven. There were seven magpies on his forearm.

A nurse put a gown on the doctor. Dr. Kelly held up his hands, and a ring shone on his finger. The rest of the nursery rhyme came to her: *Five for silver, six for gold.*

The doctor put a mask on, then his gloves.

Seven for a secret never to be told.

He leaned over her, his eyes a familiar blue. "What have we got here?"

A nurse screamed.

A voice said, "What *is* that?"

Bridget felt it coming out of her, a long rope of pain and pressure.

Somewhere in the room, wings flapped.

April's Fool is May's Corpse

The trunk is pitch black.

There's supposed to be a glow-in-the-dark handle in car trunks now, but there isn't one in here. I checked. Everywhere. I pulled up the carpeting and felt along the sides, the door, the roof, any place within my reach. I felt every inch of this trunk and didn't find anything that could possibly be the pull handle. Which means this has to be an older model car. I never saw it, other than a flash of scuffed blue paint reflecting the sun, then the darkness of the trunk.

I've been in the car at least an hour. In the beginning, I'd only felt panic and terror, from the moment they grabbed me outside the store. So many hands on me. Rough, forceful, careless. My groceries spilled across the sun-beaten pavement, the crinkling of the paper bag still going when I hit the hard, itchy carpet. Their masked faces flashed in the gap as the trunk lid closed, locking me in with the smell of motor oil and dog. The masks were those featureless, white ones that left a void in my mind where it expected to see eyes, a mouth, anything.

Not one word was spoken.

It was so fast I didn't even have time to scream until the trunk shut.

The roads were relatively smooth before now. The car's bouncing over rutted roads, rocks clunking off the underside. Already sore, I'm doing my best not to slam all around the confined space, but there's nothing to hold onto, nothing to keep me in one safe spot. Some of the holes are so big that I get bounced up to the roof. My head is throbbing. I think I dislocated a finger, but until the movement calms down, I'm afraid to touch it in case I make it worse.

I don't know why I've been kidnapped. I'm not famous. There's certainly no money, so if that's why they took me they'll find my savings account is non-existent. I had to transfer the last of it into checking just to get the wasted groceries that are now cooking in a parking lot next to the wide open trunk of my own car. Did they take my keys or has someone already driven off with my car?

No one will pay a ransom for me. My parents are long dead, I've never been married, and I have no kids. My friends don't have the funds to pay a ransom. I try to think why else they might have kidnapped me, but my mind skirts past rape and murder, afraid to dwell on it. Those seem to be the most likely reason, unless someone was dumb enough to take a random stranger and assume they'd have the money. All they need to do is take me to an ATM and I can prove that, really, it's them who should be paying me here. There's $5.63 in my checking account. Plus the $5 minimum that has to remain in my savings account. Even if they tried to force me to take that $5 out, the bank won't let it happen.

I can't even pay the rent this month. I'm about to be homeless. If I live through whatever this is. The car's paid off, at least, but it's a ticking time bomb. There's a rattling sound and some sort of heavy clunk that happens occasionally. The windshield's cracked so badly that if I were to give someone a ride they wouldn't be able to see the road through the spiderweb of breaks on the passenger side. That's what happens when a rock chip isn't treated in time, but that takes money, too.

Maybe they've taken me to force me to rob a bank. Or to do a home invasion. Considering we've left the paved roads and are now clearly traveling over dirt and gravel roads, a home invasion makes the most sense. At this point, I'd be willing to bargain for a piece of the take. Just enough to get me to the end of the week. The money's spent the moment it comes in. I got paid yesterday and it disappeared instantly because I already had payments pending. I sent a post-dated check for the rent and it's going to bounce. The utility bill is due in a week, and there's no way I can pay it.

I can't believe I'm thinking about my financial woes when I'm locked in the trunk of a moving vehicle.

Okay, collect my thoughts, yes. The trunk was barren when they dropped me in, so there's no weapon I can use. One of my shoes fell off, and they took my purse. Even if they hadn't, the deadliest thing in it was a tube of chapstick. I suppose I could figure out a way to kill them with a bedraggled tampon that's been in there far too long, the paper stripped away, the cotton puffed out and ragged. My phone's not heavy enough to cause any real damage.

I had an aunt who smacked my cousins around with her shoe whenever they made her mad, but they'd told me the sound was worse than the smack itself. It made her feel better without doing any actual harm to them. I could take off my jeans and try to hit them or strangle them with it, but there are at least three people, I think.

The car is slowing. It turns, goes another few feet, then comes to a stop.

I grab my shoe, clutch it tight in my hand. It's all I've got. I mentally prepare myself to fight and run barefoot through whatever field or forest I'm greeted with. It's going to hurt, and I need to be ready for that. It will hurt less than whatever they have planned for me, I'm sure. Panic is a living thing in my gut right now, and I try to force it down, to channel it in some way, like storing energy for the fight about to happen.

The engine turns off.

You can take a hit, I tell myself. *Whatever they do, however much it hurts, you fight. Take the hits. Hit them back. Fight.*

There's the creak of doors opening. They close with a firm finality that tells me time's almost up.

Footsteps crunch across what sounds like gravel.

A key scrapes the keyhole near me. For a moment I'd lost track of where the back of the vehicle was. It's definitely an old car if they're using a key instead of a key fob.

I roll onto my back and position the shoe to strike out as soon as the lid opens. My heart is pounding so hard I think I can hear it echoing in the trunk. I want to vomit.

Sunlight pours in through the crack. The wider it opens, the less I can see.

I kick upward to open the trunk faster, hoping it will hit someone. I can't see them other than as shadows against the bright light. Voids. I swing the shoe at the shadows, make contact, keep going, keep slapping, keep swinging. There are grunts. I kick, too, lashing out. My foot hits the edge and I hear the crunch of at least one of my toes even as I pull the leg back to kick again.

It doesn't hurt yet.

Hands grab my leg, my arm. I try to pull them back, flail them, anything to free them.

My eyes have started to adjust, and now I can see those stupid masks again. They're wearing caps to cover their hair, matching mechanic-style coveralls that are too big for them and sag, hanging shapeless.

One of them takes my shoe.

I jerk my arm free, reach for a mask. Miss it.

The gloved hands are all on me again, and they haul me out of the trunk. They plunk me down on the ground. Sharp stones cut into my soles.

One of them pushes me forward, makes me stumble, but I don't fall. There's a rundown cabin up ahead, but that's not where they take me. Instead, we take a path that goes around the cabin, deeper into the woods. There are no people sounds— no cars, no lawnmowers, no kids playing. We walk for a couple minutes across a meadow of high greenish-yellow grass until a dilapidated barn looms up ahead looking like the wrong sized breath could break free giant splinters like icicles to rain down. It sags like it's tired, dark holes showing places where the wood has rotted and fallen off.

They jab me repeatedly in the back to prod me forward. I can't tell if it's a finger or a gun, which keeps me from running. If they shoot me, it's all over. If it's a gun and I can get it from them, I might stand a chance. I bide my time. Not running is one of the hardest things I've had to do.

We reach the door. I can feel them close behind me. Something pokes into my back. One of them comes around and opens the door. A few tendrils of long, dark hair peek out from underneath the cap. Something about the way this person moves makes me think it's a woman. The formlessness of the coveralls makes it hard to tell otherwise. She doesn't appear to have a gun, which leaves two that might. I take a step back, as if I'm giving her room, which puts me in contact with one of them and makes the thing poking my back jab that much harder. Throwing my head back, I make contact with something solid, a face. This time the crunch I hear is not my own, though it does hurt to hit someone else's skull.

The object pokes harder still, and I turn into it, hoping they don't pull the trigger before I get a chance to grab it.

Blood spills down the neck of the person I headbutted. They're standing a couple steps away, bent over at the waist to let it spill out. The blood has seeped through the mask a little, giving it maroon tiger stripes on the bottom half.

The other person stands stock still, their finger jabbed into my stomach now. It's not a gun, never was a gun.

I throw a punch that lands clumsily on their cheek. The mask cracks, but doesn't come off.

I run.

The trees grow nearer. There are burrs that dig into my feet and legs, but they don't matter. The only thing that matters is getting away.

There are footsteps behind me, fast, getting closer. Their breaths sound like the coal-driven puffs of a train.

Or those could be my breaths. It's all a blur.

I veer onto the path, trying to get out of the tall grasses that drag at my legs and shoot prickles into my jeans. The path is hard, with jagged rocks poking out in places. My feet are an amalgamation of pains, both bruised and punctured. They ache.

The trees are only a few more feet. I dig down and work up as much energy as I can to speed up.

The person behind is getting closer.

There are more footsteps from my right. I don't look to see who it is.

They're gaining.

Just as I'm about to break into the darkness of the woods, something slams into me mid-back. I fly forward and hit a wide-trunked tree, its rough bark scraping my cheek and chest.

I'm down, the hard ground flying up to meet me. My head slams into it with such force that there's a bright flash of light in my vision, then darkness. I don't pass out all the way, but I wish I had, because the pain that explodes in my head is the worst I've ever felt. It feels like my brain has been punched directly, like a blood vessel has blown. I taste blood.

Rough arms grab me, and when I'm turned around I discover there are now four people. Where did the extra one come from? They join us, and I'm pushed down to the ground. Someone puts their hand on the back of my head and grinds it into the dirt. A knee digs into my back, the person's weight pushing the air out of my lungs. Rocks cut my chin and cheek. My arms are pulled back roughly and tied. I try to hold them apart, hoping I've left some room to wiggle out later.

They still haven't spoken to me, and it scares me. Do I know them? Is that why they won't speak? I ache to hear a voice.

"Why are you doing this?" I ask. I want them to talk to me. "What do you want? I don't have money."

Someone smacks the back of my head.

"Just tell me what you want and we'll figure it out."

Two of them pull me to standing by grasping my arms. They push me again, but this time there's a person on either side of me, then the two in back. They keep hold of my arms.

The door gapes open ahead. It's dark inside.

When we step through the door, cool air swirls around me.

The door swings shut behind me. It sounds like they've bolted it with a clunk of wood and the rasp of something metallic. The door didn't creak, which surprises me. As if they'd oiled it ahead of time. There's fresh straw on the ground. A lone chair sits up ahead, a rolling cart next to it. There are straps on the two front legs and the armrests of the chair.

That chair's meant for me. I'm certain that if I let them strap me in, I will not be getting out of it again. Not in one piece.

But why? I don't remember doing anything to piss someone off enough to want to torture me. There's no reason anyone should hate me this much. I keep my head down, do my work, pay my bills when I'm able. Was I a random victim to give them their thrills or was I targeted? I wish they'd talk to me.

We're close enough to the cart now for me to be able to see what's sitting on it. I don't recognize half of the implements, but they all look brutal. Some sharp, some hooked, some heavy. There's a scalpel, pliers, a screwdriver, a knife, a hammer, a hatchet. A syringe and some sort of liquid in a small bottle sit next to it all. There's a tape recorder. I didn't know anyone had those anymore. Everything but the tape recorder looks like it's intended for slow torture. The hatchet's the biggest thing sitting there. While they could probably kill me with half the items, something tells me it won't be that quick.

I resist the urge to fight right then and there. No way am I letting them strap me down. I have to get away. The transition into the chair and when they're trying to strap me in should be the hardest time for them to keep a solid hold of me. That is when I will act.

My body tenses up in preparation.

One of them tightens their grip as if they felt the change in my body.

My heart is pounding, pumping blood throughout my body so I can run. In the split second before they start to turn me so I can sit back in the chair, adrenaline spurts into my bloodstream. I can feel it's power, my power.

Sure enough, one set of hands loosens as they all begin to change position to strap me down.

I kick sideways and back toward the one with the hardest grip. My foot connects, and those hands are off me. I wrench my body as hard as I can, and the second grip falters. Remembering something I saw on some news show, I rub my hands together rapidly and repeatedly. The rope slides free, but not before burning my wrists.

One of them tackles me, taking me to the ground. I'm on my stomach; they're on my back.

I'm not staying down this time.

I try the headbutt maneuver again. I miss completely. I arch backward and buck instead, throwing them off.

One of them stands over me, so I grab their leg and push up, knocking them off their feet.

I stand up, look around to get my bearings. Two are on the ground, two approaching me, their arms out like people do when they're trying to corner and catch an animal. If they want an animal, I will give them an animal.

From the cart I grab the hammer. I scream and run at the closest person, swinging the hammer in a wide arc. It connects with their head, sounding like a walnut cracking, but duller. I'm yelling. I can hear it, but I can't stop it. I swing the hammer at one of the people on the ground, hear a bone break in their arm when I make contact.

I pick up the hatchet, too. They still outnumber me.

"Wait!" yells one. "This isn't what you think."

I've always hated that line in movies, thinking no one would actually use it. Pissed off about the situation, but also their use of a stupid line, I swing the hatchet. It plunges into their chest with a solid squelch reminiscent of chopping beef. I can't pull it back out.

I can't tell if what is feeding me is anger or fear. I think it's both. My face is hot, my heart pounding, my mouth dry. Everything feels so sped up that it's in slow motion, which doesn't make sense, but it *is* how it feels. I'm going to die in this barn in the middle of the woods if I don't finish the job. I need to get the car keys, make a break for it. One of them has to have a phone.

"Hannah!" one screams. So they know my name. They targeted me on purpose.

I swing the hammer at the only one left standing, feel it connect. I'm already looking to see who poses the most danger. One is getting up off the ground. They see me coming and freeze, holding up one hand. "Hannah, it's me. It's Suzy."

That doesn't make sense. Suzy wouldn't do this. I walk toward the person claiming to be my best friend. We've been friends since elementary school. There's no way she'd attack me.

The voice sounds an awful lot like hers.

She sobs. "Hannah, please." She takes off the mask.

It *is* Suzy. Her nose is off-kilter, blood drying on the bottom half of her face. The one I headbutted. She stands up slowly, hands still held out.

I'm frozen in place, looking around at the others. If that's Suzy, the others have to be the rest of our ladies' night crew.

Sure enough, they all take their masks off. All, that is, except the one I put the hatchet through. That one's lying on the ground, unmoving. Blood darkens the front of their coveralls. The other two are revealed to be Amy and Ratna. That leaves the hatchet victim to be Sheryl.

"Why did you do this?" I ask. Hurt replaces the fear. My stomach turns, feeling greasy. My chest hurts.

"We weren't going to hurt you. Press play on the tape."

They're staying where they are, giving me space. I press the button and listen to the staticky voices calling out together, "April Fools!"

Don't they see that I've killed somebody now? There's no going back. I'm going to be arrested, imprisoned. I'm a murderer. This time I do throw up. I can't stop it from coming up. My life is over. They thought this would be funny? How long were they planning this, acting to my face like nothing was going on?

I think about what my future looks like. My face on the news. The judgment. A jury denying self-defense. My job firing me. People crossing the street to avoid me. Neighbors staring at me through their windows, unwilling to come near. Prison time. All the awful things that happen in prison.

I think about my own friends hurting me. They hit me, tackled me, shoved me into a trunk. I can feel all the pain in my body throbbing. My cut up feet, my busted finger, the pulsating pain in my skull.

I have to finish it now. There can't be any witnesses.

As I kill my closet friends, I repeat, "April Fools, April Fools, April Fools..."

The Hunt

Mina ran her hands over the ridiculous uniform one more time to make sure nothing was amiss. It was a standard maid's uniform, a shapeless dress with a small apron like the ones she'd seen in movies, but instead of the grey and white she expected, it was pastel pink and mint green. She felt like something rejected from a bag of candy.

This was her first temp position. She'd expected something more along the lines of a conference at a hotel, serving plated dinners, but as far as she understood, she'd be working a banquet at an Easter egg hunt in this atrocious McMansion. It had turrets and columns and garage doors that resembled carriage house doors, with slabs of wood crossed on the fronts of each individual one. Details she might have loved were they done in a different way were collaged across a stucco façade like a smorgasbord of poor taste. It was gaudy and tacky. Everything she'd come to expect from the stupidly rich.

They had told her to park on the side in a lot with rundown vehicles much like hers. The side entrance wasn't visible to the folks arriving for the party, so no one had to acknowledge there were plebs waiting to serve them. How anyone was supposed to be invisible in pastels was a mystery to Mina, but she approached the side entrance in the high heels the agency had told her to wear. Another surprise, considering she'd have to be on her feet the entire time. The agency said the shoes were required. No sensible flats, no sneakers. In short, nothing that could make getting through this shift any easier.

Sometimes she wondered if the cancer treatments had been worth it. She'd be paying all of it off for the rest of her life, and it struck her sometimes that she'd literally saved her life only to spend the rest of it paying off having done so. Part of her kept reminding herself, in a voice that sounded an awful lot like her mother's, that she should just be happy to be alive. And she was. Most days.

It took a minute for someone to answer her knock on the door. When it opened, an honest to god butler stood in the doorway, coattails and all, in the same pastels she wore. He still managed to look dignified, and she decided to take a page from his book, lifting her chin high and nodding her thanks to him. If he could pull off Easter bunny vomit, so could she.

"Cell phone." He held out his white gloved hand. There was a certain amount of dissonance for her that he had an American accent instead of a British one.

"I left it in the car," she responded. "Like the instructions said."

"Great. This way for the party preparations."

He led her through the house to a kitchen in the rear. It was dark, with only one window, and industrial stainless-steel appliances. The cabinets were white and so clean they practically sparkled. Even with about fifteen bodies rushing around, some in chef's garb, some in the same uniform as her, the floor and counters were spotless. Her kitchen didn't even look this tidy after she'd cleaned it. Not even after a week of eating fast food and therefore hardly using the kitchen. It was astonishing.

The butler cleared his throat. "Grab one of the platters and follow me. I'll show you where we're setting up, and then you can help bring the rest of the platters out."

Mina grabbed a large, silver platter full of some kind of meat-filled pastries and followed the butler down a hallway that led to what appeared to be a side exit to a giant backyard. There were animal-shaped bushes and somehow the grass was green despite it being early spring. It should have been brown. They walked along a path that eventually led to a series of banquet-sized rectangular tables already lined with a significant amount of food, including some amazing desserts. What looked to be two entire lambs sat at the very center, a visual focal point. Two gravy boats full of mint jelly sat on either side of the massive platter. The tables bore white tablecloths and stretched for several yards, looking down on a multi-terraced and gorgeously landscaped yard that included a pool. Massive square hedges outlined the yard, with no other houses visible, though she'd passed some getting here.

She set her platter down and jogged to catch up to the butler, not sure she could find her way back to the kitchen just yet. Her heels clacked on the paving stones. He looked back at her and shook his head, but didn't say anything. It didn't take long to get to the kitchen, and Mina didn't have any further problems getting back and forth between the tables and the kitchen, smiling at other similarly dressed women who were making the same journey.

When she returned to the kitchen only to find that all platters had been put out and the butler had disappeared, she looked around frantically for someone to ask for the next steps. A chef looked at her with sympathy and tilted his chin toward the hallway. "Back out to the tables."

"Thanks."

Moving quickly, she got back out to the banquet setup and stepped into line with the other servers, who had been arranged behind the tables about a foot apart, facing up toward the back of the house, their backs to the lower terraces. She got settled just in time, as a wave of sound came down from the back of the mansion, a horde of adults spilling from the ornate glass doors lining the back wall. There was a slight slope between the doors and the tables, and two cobble-stoned paths leading down toward the table level.

Mina was taken aback to see the adults, expecting a bunch of toddlers and young kids, but she'd long heard the rich were different, and it was definitely true in this case. If grown-ass rich people wanted to hunt for Easter eggs, who was she to judge?

The adults were dressed in their Sunday best clothes, down to pearls, sweater vests, and dress shoes. As they poured down the paths to reach the tables, one woman twisted her ankle and went down. She stood right back up and hobbled onward, the others parting around her in order to pass. She kept limping along, tears creating streams of mascara down her cheeks, dark droplets splattering across her robin's egg blue sheath dress.

Up on the second-floor porch that stretched along the entire length of the mansion, a woman wearing a summer dress the color of egg yolk stepped grandly out of the central door of three and walked to the railing, placing her hands on it. Her white hair had been swept up into a high bouffant with a golden clip that sparkled in the sunshine. Four other people, two men and two women, came out and stood to either side of her. They wore bright shades of blue, green, pink, and orange, the men in suits, the women in dresses.

The crowd surged past the tables to the tier below, ignoring the food.

The butler walked along the tables behind the servers and quietly spoke to each woman, who moved around to the other side of the table, facing down toward the lower tiers. Mina considered going before he got to her, but no one else was doing so, and she figured it was all part of whatever weird show they were putting on for the people on the porch. She waited until he reached her, when he said, "Go ahead," then she followed the woman to her left around to the other side.

Now that she could see the next tier down, things that had barely registered as she ran back and forth from the kitchen now caught her attention. There were several large items covered under white tarps. The egg hunters had crowded together around these and milled about restlessly, staring up at the woman on the porch.

"Welcome," the woman's voice boomed from off to the left, startling Mina. She hadn't noticed the nearby speaker. Now that she saw it, others materialized in her vision, positioned around the grounds. "This is the fifth annual Helton family Easter egg hunt."

The crowd cheered.

"As you know, the prize is two-million dollars for the finder of the crystal egg."

Another cheer.

"There are no rules other than that the hunt remains outside and on these grounds. Do not stray from the property. Do not go into the house. The victorious hunter gets the prize." The woman now peered down at the butler. "Webster, when you're ready."

The butler, Webster apparently, stepped forward from the center of the table and pointed a small pistol into the air at an angle. He fired off one shot and mayhem ensued below.

The hunters, as the woman had called them, ran in all directions, a boiling mass of pastels. They ripped the tarps off the large items and revealed weapons Mina had only ever seen in movies. There were spears, bows, crossbows, baseball bats, axes, machetes, swords, knives, throwing stars, and items she couldn't identify. All the metal sparkled in the spring sun. Even more so as the hunters grabbed what they could and ran.

Mina looked around to see what everyone else was doing. This couldn't be real. But everyone on the serving staff stared straight ahead as if nothing were happening.

What *was* happening?

A woman wearing oversized pearls, her hair up in a bun, swiped at a man with a machete. Blood sprayed from his chest. He slapped a hand to his chest and swung his bat with the other. The woman ducked and came up, the machete arcing upward straight into his groin. He fell to the ground, trying to cover his wounds.

The woman ran on toward someone else.

Two men squared off not far from the last battle. One held a crossbow, which he pointed at the other man, who held a spear. The spear swung into the crossbow, loosing an arrow, which flew up in a graceful arc, coming down into the forehead of a server just two spaces away from Mina. The server's knees buckled, and she slumped to the ground, seizing. The women on either side of her moved away slightly, but continued to look ahead.

It wasn't safe to stand here. Mina took a step forward, but an iron grip fell upon her arm. She looked down at the hand and traced it up to the owner, the woman to her right. The woman shook her head, squeezed, then let go. "Don't," she whispered.

Down the line, a server bolted. Mina watched her, ready to

29

run, as well, but before the woman got past the end of the table, her head exploded, the sound of the gunshot following. Blood still misted the air for a moment after her body hit the ground. Webster turned back to the battle below and placed the handgun in its holster, under his jacket.

"What is this?" Mina whispered.

"It's an Easter egg hunt," the woman who'd stopped her replied.

"That is the last thing this is."

"We shouldn't be talking. They tip well if you stay put. Now just stand still, serve the food when someone comes along, and finish out your shift. And shut up before you get us both killed."

Webster glanced their way. He placed a hand on his gun.

Mina looked straight ahead, her body quaking. She tried to use her peripheral vision to see him, but he was too far away.

Sweat broke out on her palms. She wiped them on her uniform.

Below, the mayhem continued. Grunts, blood flying, screams.

After a moment, she risked peeking toward Webster. He no longer looked at her. She let out her held breath and forced her shoulders to relax. The server had said they tipped, which meant they let the staff go at the end. Or so it seemed. Maybe she'd misunderstood.

"So they let us go?"

"Shhhh."

A man chucked a spear at a woman whose back was turned to him. It hit her in the thigh and she shrieked in agony, refusing to fall to the ground. She tried to pull it out, but couldn't.

The man ran over and grabbed the spear, tearing it from her thigh.

She hacked at him with a knife, but missed.

He pulled back the spear and jabbed it through her stomach. The tip popped out through her back.

The woman grabbed the wooden handle and slumped over, once more trying to remove it, but he kept a strong grip on it and started pulling it back. Her screams rose above the rest of the noise, louder than the grunts and yells, the meaty sounds of bodily injuries.

"Finish her!" yelled one of the people on the porch.

Mina started to turn, to see who had yelled, but the server next to her spoke once more. "Stop. Don't respond. Don't turn."

"Why are you helping me?" Mina asked.

"If he shoots at you, there's a good chance he'll hit me."

That was definitely not what Mina had expected. Here she thought the woman cared if she lived or died.

The man couldn't get the spear out, so he wrested the knife away from the woman and slit her throat.

Mina gasped. It was all so brutal. The money didn't seem worth it. Not at this cost. The green of the grass had disappeared under blood, gore, and bodies. The pastels of these people's clothing were coated in the deep red of blood.

"What's your name?" Mina whispered. She needed something to hold onto, some handle of normalcy.

"Sandy. Now shut it."

Webster walked their way. He was in front of the tables, while they were behind them. He studied each woman as he passed.

Mina stiffened her body and waited for him to get to her.

He stopped in front of her, eyes squinted. His hands were behind his back, which meant they weren't on the gun. He looked harmless, like the usual stuffed-shirt butler, but she knew it was deceptive. This man would kill her if she breathed wrong. He wouldn't even hesitate.

Mina didn't know what to do. He was so intense, his gaze not leaving her. Finally, she allowed her eyes to meet his and nodded.

He nodded back and moved on.

She still wasn't sure it had been the right thing to do. The last thing she should be doing is drawing his attention, but it had seemed like he was waiting for something. *They're going to let you go home and they're going to tip you.* Mina said this over and over in her head. *You get to go home. This is okay.*

Not a single word of it felt like the truth.

Webster crossed back in front of them, having reached the end of the tables. He kept going until he reached the other end, then turned back and returned to his place at the center of the table. He fired into the air again.

Below, everyone stopped fighting. There were bodies in various states of battle. A woman had mounted another woman, hands wrapped around her throat. Two men sliced at each other repeatedly with knives, both bleeding profusely, seeming to be too weak to move away to safety. A man and woman beat each other with clubs, darting around a large shrub shaped like what appeared to be a bear. A man hacked another man with an axe, despite his clearly already being dead. Two women wrestled in the pool, a cloud of blood surrounding them.

All of them stopped at the sound of the gun.

"That's lunch," called Webster.

Battered and bleeding, each individual came toward the table, most of them limping or impaired in some way. A man, his right arm missing, came along with them. He tucked a couple throwing stars into his pants pocket, blood leaking through the khaki material in spots.

No one touched anyone else. They hardly glanced at each other.

They grabbed delicate white bone china plates from either end of the table and started down the line. The servers removed metal domes from over their dishes, steam rising, along with the smells of food. The scents of butter, garlic, and rosemary wafted up to Mina, but when the first person reached her, the odors of urine and blood covered it up. She dished up baby potatoes and buttered asparagus, working hard to not gag or show her disgust in any way.

Up close, there were astonishing wounds. Wounds that didn't seem to belong on living humans. A woman's scalp hung partially over her face, white bone visible where her skull had been exposed. A man had bone sticking through his bicep. Another woman sported a giant gash in her daisy yellow sweater from which a small loop of intestine hung. She kept pushing at it mindlessly, accompanied by wet sounds.

It was all too much. The only thing keeping Mina from screaming and running away was her strong desire to live. She would not die on her first temp assignment with the banquet company. They must have known what they were sending her to. What was the requirement to be sent to this job? Debt?

Unless no one had ever reported this to them. That didn't seem possible. None of this seemed real. This mansion was in the middle of an upper-class suburbia. The neighbors had to hear the gunshots.

A warbling voice came up from somewhere on the lower tier. "My leg. I need help."

Mina resisted the urge to look around. She already knew no one would respond. No one would even look in that direction. She'd done enough to call attention to herself. It was time to start acting like everyone else if she had any hope of making it home to her shitty apartment. She would sure as hell be vetting assignments more stringently from here on out. She smiled and doled out glistening baby potatoes to a man with a sucking chest wound, blood running down his arm and pooling on the stark white of the porcelain plate, soaking his food.

He smiled back.

These people were like crazy robots or something. They should all be clamoring for help, for escape, for assistance. For something. Taking a lunch break in the middle of slaughtering each other struck Mina as surreal. They were going to sit down next to people who were either going to kill them or be killed by them. Their number had already dwindled by at least half, and it seemed like more than half to Mina, but she hadn't bothered to count them when they first ran down from the house.

There were round tables off to the side, all with the same white tablecloths and decorative white lawn chairs. As each individual finished making their way down the buffet line, they went to the tables and picked a chair. Soon they were engaged in what looked like earnest conversations. Bright red blood smeared across the linens and chairs until everything looked like it was made of red and white dalmatian skin.

Around her, the servers put the covers back on the platters. Mina did the same. As she tucked the serving tongs under a cover, she noticed a smear of blood on the tablecloth. Her stomach rolled. She couldn't stop looking at it, a deep red slash across the crisp white, so she ever so slightly shifted a platter to cover the smear.

She'd been so transfixed by the blood and making it go away, that she hadn't seen Webster approaching. His shadow fell over the table and she slowly lifted her eyes to his, afraid of what she would see.

He nodded. "You learn fast."

She didn't dare smile, merely nodding in return. His lips tilted in a slight smile and he moved on.

Mina took a moment to turn her head just enough to get the round tables within her sight and counted them now. There were twelve people remaining. She could have sworn the original number was around forty, but perhaps she had exaggerated in her head. If she were right, that would mean there were twenty-eight dead people somewhere on the expansive lawns of this place. Visible lumps were spread across the tiered lawns. A couple appeared to still be alive, though barely, small movements occurring. One man's foot twitched several times before stilling.

A moan sounded from the same direction as the leg person. Then wet sobs. A cough.

She tried to process how long they'd been down there fighting. It couldn't have been long. Her feet were barely tired. Her heels were still steady on the stone patio, and she was deeply out of practice in wearing high heels. She should have been wobbling within an hour, which meant it hadn't even been an hour yet of witnessing this savagery. It felt interminable.

It can't be more than another hour and then you can go home, she told herself.

Even an hour was a long time.

A gunshot startled Mina, and she realized she'd been so intently in her own head that she'd missed everyone at the round tables standing up. Webster must have let them know it was time. With the gunshot, they all poured back down toward the battlefield full of corpses, searching out weapons to get back into the fight. One woman wrenched an axe out of a corpse and let out a guttural yell as she ran for two people who were engaged in hand-to-hand combat. She swung it wide and slammed it into a man's neck. When she pulled it out, blood spurted in a torrent. Before his body hit the ground, she'd swung the axe into a woman's face. She tried to pull it out, but it stuck, so she ran to look for another weapon. That was two people down already.

They certainly weren't the last.

The violence continued, and still the servers were made to stand there and watch. Shouldn't they be cleaning up by now? It seemed odd for them to want them to stay the entire time. She risked a glance toward Webster and found him standing in his place at the center of the table. A wind came up and blew his jacket back, revealing the gun in its holster. The wind also chilled the dampness under her arms. She hoped her deodorant would hold out.

Down on the next tier of the yard, there were only eight remaining combatants. One man sported three throwing stars, two jutting from his chest, one sticking out of his forehead. He fought with a sword, making wide, fast sweeps with it. It looked heavy, cumbersome. The woman he fought was agile, leaping away from the blade each time. As he recovered from a particularly large swipe, she brought up her machete and swung at his neck. He moved at the last minute. The blade went into his shoulder. She tried to pull it out, lifting one foot up to press against his stomach for leverage.

An arrow sailed out of nowhere and embedded itself in the woman's back. She let go of the machete and reached back for the arrow, but couldn't get to it.

Another arrow hit the man in the chest. He crumpled.

A third arrow hit the woman in the throat.

A fourth went in around her ear.

She tried to run, but nothing on her body seemed to work correctly. Fighting to breathe past the arrow, she clawed at her throat, stumbling, one leg dragging.

From behind Mina, someone on the porch laughed.

A fifth arrow slammed into the combatant's eye. She stiffened. One hand came up, grasped the arrow, and pulled. Her other joined it, yanking.

The woman plopped down on her butt, legs splayed, and continued to pull.

She struggled for an interminable amount of time. Mina couldn't drag her eyes away.

An odd sense of relief flooded Mina when the woman collapsed. Horrified, yet impressed at the woman's stoicism and drive, Mina had been holding her breath. Her hands shook, so she grasped them in front of her, trying to look professional while at the same time holding them still. How could the others deal with this? How could they have come back more than once? No amount of money was worth this. All she wanted was to go home.

"You're hyperventilating," Sandy whispered. "You'll catch someone's attention."

Mina hadn't even realized she was breathing heavy. She'd been holding it just a moment ago. Taking a deep, steadying breath, she focused on keeping it normal. These people would kill her in a hot second if she stepped out of line. Well, they'd stand by and have Webster do it. All this for their entertainment. Ever since the cancer treatments she'd been good at focusing on her breathing and blocking other things out, yet she was struggling to do the same here. This was too horrific to dissociate from.

She wondered if anyone had tried going to the cops before. If someone had ever left and reported what had happened. Maybe they had and no one had believed them. Maybe the local officials had been paid off. Money greased a lot of wheels. Everyone understood that, but it struck her that perhaps not many understood how bad it really was. Surely someone had tried and failed if this was an annual event. The question was, what had happened to the person reporting it?

Dragged from her thoughts by an angry, high-pitched shriek, Mina found there were only two contenders remaining. The bloodied pastel queens circled each other. Whereas they'd been dressed to the nines, their makeup perfect, hair coiffed, when they arrived, they both now sported ragged hair, frizz hanging in their faces. Mascara and lipstick had smeared, making them almost clown-like. Their previously pristine dress clothes were now torn, bloodied, and filthy. They both had wicked looking daggers, which they swiped at each other repeatedly, drawing small amounts of blood with each cut. At this rate, it would be death by a thousand cuts for them.

The brunette threw herself at the blonde, knocking the other woman to the ground. As the blonde fell, she struck out with her knife, slashing it across the brunette's throat. Blood sprayed the blonde's face, coating her in a fresh coat of crimson to cover the rusty browns and shades of red already on her clothes.

Mouth gaping like a fish's as it drowns in the open air, the brunette used both hands to bring the knife down into the blonde's chest. She did this three more times before collapsing on the woman below her.

Neither woman moved.

Nobody at all moved.

It felt like five minutes before Webster stirred, walking down a small set of stairs to the battlefield. He knelt and took each woman's wrist. The breeze stirred his hair, soughing through the hedges and making them dance.

Mina took the opportunity to look back at the porch. Everyone still stood at the railing, their faces intent as they watched Webster. She turned away before any of them could notice. Or so she hoped.

Sandy sighed. It rankled Mina. Her weird act of being the murder police was getting annoying. It appeared she held more judgment for Mina being curious and freaked out than about the absolute brutality that had occurred around them.

Webster stood up, looked up at the porch, and shook his head.

Several silent moments passed.

The woman spoke from the porch. "The servers will now compete for the prize. At the first shot, find your weapons."

It took a second for Mina to process what had been said. Then her stomach flooded and nausea hit. She choked back the vomit making its way up her throat. Looking around, she saw the same level of confusion in everyone else. It looked like this was a first for them, too, which didn't reassure Mina.

They couldn't do this. No one could force her to fight for her life. She eyeballed the pathway, measuring the distance from her place at the serving table to the corner of the building. It was probably 500 feet away. She could make it.

The server on the end nearest the pathway back to the kitchen bolted.

A shot rang out.

The server went down. Webster kept the gun out, pointed it upward, and fired again.

The women around her broke away from the table. Except

one, who fell to her feet and threw up.

Another server turned around, ran back to the table and looked around. Not finding a suitable weapon, the woman took off her heels and slashed the vomiting woman across the face. The cut woman wailed and vomited once more. The attacker looked up at the porch, held the high heels up, and proceeded to beat the other woman with them repeatedly, gouging her flesh and bursting an eyeball, the viscous fluid oozing down her cheek and splattering the weapon-wielder.

Eventually, the woman on the ground stopped screaming.

Mina looked at the table before her. There were no knives nearby, only tongs, dishes, and spoons. She grabbed the large, silver platter and cover from in front of her, one in each hand, kicked off her heels, and ran for the lower tier. She needed a better weapon, and fast. Cancer hadn't beaten her. Neither would these women.

The smell reached her as she ran down the steps. It smelled like a clogged toilet full of shit, combined with the heavy, metallic scent of blood. She slipped as her foot hit the blood-slicked grass, but kept her feet. There were bodies everywhere, some with the weapons still stuck in them. It was a minefield of corpses, clogging the yard.

Before her, the women had already engaged, grabbing whatever weapon they came across. There were only six women aside from her.

Only? She didn't want to kill one woman, let alone six.

Her heart pounded and panic blurred her vision. She blinked to clear her eyes.

A banshee shriek came from Mina's right. She pivoted just in time, holding up the lid to block the bat swinging toward her. It hit with a loud *bong* that sent pain shooting up her hand and arm. She nearly dropped the lid, the nerves in her hand screaming.

The woman swung again.

This time, Mina blocked the swing, pushing past the agony of a second hit, and swung the platter. Her grip on it was questionable, but it made contact with the woman's head hard enough to knock her back a couple steps.

Mina's hand gave out. The platter fell to the grass. She still clutched the lid.

She turned and ran, searching for a free weapon.

Footsteps pounded behind her.

A puff of air whistled at the back of her head. The bat had just missed her.

Up ahead, on the other side of two women locked in battle with swords they could barely lift, was a hatchet. Mina darted behind one of the women, barely evading a blade as the woman hefted her sword in preparation for a swing. Mina dove to the ground, but fell just short of being able to reach the hatchet.

She had a split second to decide whether to crawl forward for the hatchet or turn onto her back to face her attacker. Thinking of how close the bat had come as she ran, she flipped over, holding the lid up in front of her.

The woman, face contorted was on her in a second, swinging the bat down toward Mina's head.

Mina blocked it and kicked out, her foot hitting the other woman's knee. An awful *crack* sounded and the woman's leg buckled. She screamed, but didn't let go of the bat.

Pushing up onto one forearm, the woman swung the bat and hit Mina in the ankle. It didn't have the heft it would have were she standing, but it still sent pain crashing across Mina's foot and leg. She kicked again, this time connecting with the woman's face.

With her attacker down, Mina turned over and scrambled on hands and knees to the hatchet, snatching it up. She stood and faced the woman who had attacked her.

The woman rose up onto one leg, favoring the other. She held the bat with two hands and swung it twice to show she could. "That hatchet's pretty short. Think you can get me before I get you?"

Mina felt zero confidence, but figured running away and not engaging would get her shot. Webster stood on the upper level of the yard, in front of the tables, where he'd been before. He seemed to sense what Mina was thinking and placed his hand on the butt of his gun, meeting her eyes.

Forward it was, then.

A fresh hit of adrenaline coursed through her veins, and Mina ran forward, hatchet held up.

The woman got into position, turning slightly to the side and raising the bat to chest level.

Mina threw the lid at the woman, who swung at it. It meant she wasn't in position to swing at Mina anymore, which registered on her face in a widening of the eyes and mouth just as Mina brought the hatchet down into her head.

It surprised Mina how solid the skull felt when the hatchet came down on it.

Blood poured down the woman's face, going into her eyes. Blinded, she swung, but it was too clumsy and missed Mina.

Mina brought the hatchet down again, this time with more force. She felt it break through the skull, heard the crack, and saw it sink in. More blood came down in a sheet.

The woman still swung the bat, but it was mindless now. She ran down like a bad clock and slumped to the ground, fingers twitching.

This time, Mina couldn't hold back the vomit. In that split second, she was no longer fighting for her life, and the reality of what she'd just done set in. She had killed a woman. It felt senseless, and yet she didn't feel she had a choice. She kept her feet, but bent over to heave her meager stomach contents onto the grass.

One of the women they'd passed ran the other one through with her sword. It passed right out the back. The stabbed woman dropped her sword and grabbed the one sticking through her. Blood ran from her hands down the blade, but still she held on.

The other woman drew the sword back out, slicing through the hands gripping the blade. She kicked her opponent in the stomach and sent her to the ground.

Then she turned toward Mina.

"Shit," Mina said. She wiped her mouth on her sleeve.

In a flash of inspiration, Mina ran toward the woman, hatchet held high. Her arm was starting to tire, but she knew it would be her end if she dropped the weapon.

The woman planted herself and tried to raise the sword, but she'd been wielding it a long time, longer than Mina and the hatchet, and her arms were clearly tired.

Mina wasn't underestimating her, though. At the last

minute, well out of the sword's arc, she diverted to the right and ran around the woman. It was clear the woman would follow, but Mina had a plan. The closer she could get to the pathway, while making it appear she was in the fight, the better a chance she'd have to get out.

White hot pain shot up her spine as the sword's blade sliced into her back. It was a glancing blow, but it scared her into zagging to the left so she could turn around while evading another cut.

Desperate, she threw the axe, knowing the chances it would land right were slim.

Yet it did, embedding itself in the woman's chest with a meaty *thunk*. The woman ran forward a couple more steps, froze, and plunked down on her butt in the grass.

Mina left her to her shock. She needed another weapon, but first she needed to take stock of the situation. Only two women still stood. One was Sandy, who held a bloodied machete. The other woman held the crossbow, but only appeared to have a single arrow, which she held in one hand.

The two eyeballed each other, then the other woman dropped the crossbow and ran forward, arrow brandished the way she would have held a knife.

Sandy easily cut her down with the machete.

And then there were two.

As annoying as Sandy had become with her judgments, she had helped Mina the best she could. If it weren't for her, Mina probably would have tried to run in the beginning and been shot down for it. It felt wrong to now attack her savior, pain though she might be.

Mina made a pointed search of her surroundings, hoping it would look like she was seeking a weapon. She was, but mostly she was trying to figure out how to get closer to the exit. Sandy had returned to work this event more than once, which told Mina she had the capacity to shut down her horror. It seemed to Mina that this also meant the woman would have no problem killing her, whether she'd helped her earlier or not. So a real weapon was necessary for defense, exit or no exit.

There, in the grass not far from the steps, was a body that looked like a pincushion. It was the man with the throwing stars and arrows, who she'd watched die earlier. Not far from him was a bow.

She went for it.

If she could get up those steps with the weapons, she could lead Sandy toward the exit. Maybe the woman would escape with Mina. There was no way to know unless she tried.

Sandy had been far enough away that there was a healthy distance for her to cover. Mina looked back and found Sandy was fast. There wouldn't be much time to grab the weapons and get up the stairs. Mina took stock of what she needed to grab.

She reached the bow first and leaned down without stopping to snatch it up.

A few more steps, and she was at the man's body. It proved harder to get the arrow out than she'd expected, and she ended up having to use both hands, wasting precious seconds.

Sandy gained, now only about three yards away.

Mina managed to get the two throwing stars out of the man's chest, but left the third one in his head.

Sandy was a yard away.

Mina let out a startled yell and ran up the stairs, stuffing the throwing stars into her apron. She got up to the next level and turned to her left, toward the kitchen. As she ran, she fumbled with the arrow, trying to get it into position.

She pressed her luck as hard as she could, stopping at the end of the table to turn back and aim the bow at the savage coming up behind her. Behind Sandy, Webster had pulled his gun. He wasn't as stupid as Mina needed him to be.

Mina let the arrow fly, intending to miss Sandy, but make it look good. Instead, the arrow flew true, going into Sandy's leg.

The other woman didn't even stumble. The arrow vibrated as Sandy ran forward, machete held high.

Mina pulled out the throwing stars, now doubting everything she'd done up to this point. The exit to safety was still too far. Webster watched, gun in hand.

Sandy came at her, bloodthirsty. This woman was never going to let Mina go.

The first star missed Sandy completely. Mina tried again.

She missed again.

Unarmed, Mina saw her death coming at a rapid run. Sun

glinted off the blade of the machete.

The table. There had to be something usable on the table. Mina ran behind it, hoping to keep some space between them. She tossed the lids off various platters, seeking anything that might prove to be fatal. Everything she came across was useless.

Mina quickly lost hope.

Sandy reached the other side of the table and jabbed the machete at Mina. Mina jumped back. Then she ran immediately forward, picked up a heavy bowl, and chucked it at Sandy, who batted it away with her free hand.

Mina continued grabbing anything that looked heavy so she could throw it at the other woman. It kept Sandy distracted so she couldn't swing the machete, but it wasn't going to end the battle.

When she reached the next table, Mina threw another bowl, then grasped the table and flipped it at Sandy. It separated them a little more and allowed her to get to the next table, where she finally found a bread knife, the ridges wicked looking. It was long and slim, and the best Mina could hope for.

Sandy pulled the table out enough to step around it and arrive on the same side as Mina. "Give it up, new girl. You don't stand a chance with that little knife."

Sandy didn't know that this wasn't the first time Mina had fought for her life. That first battle had been against her own body, which had turned on her. She had won against her very cells. At least now she could see what she was fighting, could attack it physically instead of with chemicals and stubbornness.

Mina wasn't going to go down easy.

She planted her feet and waited for Sandy to get close, watching the other woman's eyes.

Sandy got to within striking distance.

"You don't have to do this," Mina said. "We could try to escape."

"I *want* to do this."

That was it then.

Sandy held the machete up and stepped forward, her gaze moving down toward Mina's throat, telegraphing her swing.

Mina stepped into the swing, throwing out one hand. She knocked the swinging arm to the side, grabbed Sandy's upper arm, and put her body in too close to Sandy for the other woman to be able to get her with the blade. Mina shoved the knife into Sandy's stomach, sickened by the smooth way it sunk into the woman's body. This wasn't a stabbing knife, so instead of pulling it out, Mina sawed and twisted it until she hit a rib and couldn't go any further.

The two stared into each other's eyes. Mina saw the moment Sandy's eyes went blank, stepping back and releasing the knife so the woman could fall to the ground.

Mina felt no satisfaction. But she did feel relief. She was alive.

"Well done, young lady. Now you have only to find the egg." The woman on the porch took a sip of wine and waved a careless hand at the yard.

"I just want to go home," Mina called up to her.

"Find the egg or Webster will finish you."

All of the strength went out of Mina's body. She sunk to her knees and sobbed, hands covering her face. She didn't care about the money. What she cared about was her freedom, her life. Her entire body was sticky with blood, with too many aches to count.

A pair of shined black shoes stepped into her sightline.

"I'm going," she yelled. "Give me a minute."

"I'm afraid you don't have a minute. Boring the mistress is not a good idea." Webster didn't sound entirely unsympathetic.

Mina looked up and found that Webster had extended a hand to help her up. She took his hand, the glove surprisingly soft against her skin, and allowed him to pull her to standing. She stepped to the edge of the terrace and looked down. Where would the egg be? She didn't even know what it would look like or what size it was. Nothing stood out on the lower tiers. There weren't any obvious hiding places.

"Getting colder," one of the men shouted from the porch.

The group tittered in reply.

Mina turned to face the people on the porch, to see if perhaps there was an egg visible up there. Nothing obvious showed itself. One of the women held her glass aloft as if to toast, then downed the red liquid inside.

The lambs caught Mina's eye. What remained of them, their

carcasses picked halfway clean.

The centerpiece of the entire table, two lambs on tall platters, and between them, a crystal egg the size of a grapefruit.

Mina limped along the table until she reached the lambs and picked up the heavy egg. Blood smeared across it from her hands, marring the polished surface. She wasn't sure if it was her blood or someone else's. Exhausted, confused, likely going into shock, she tried to clean off the egg and her hands on her uniform.

Webster stepped up next to her and held out his hands for the egg. Mina handed it over. He placed it back on the table and reached under the table, pulling a satchel out from under the ground-length tablecloth. "Your reward," he stated, handing the bag over.

Mina took the bag, but didn't bother opening it. She saluted Webster, threw another salute at the psychos standing on the porch and limped toward the pathway and the exit that would take her to her waiting car. She was thirsty and in pain, and could think of nothing but getting to her car. The grass whispered softly under her bare feet.

She knew that at any moment, there might be a gunshot. That it might have all been a trick, and they wouldn't let her leave.

Walking forward and not looking back was one of the hardest things she'd done. Not the hardest. Not by far. But certainly a show of willpower like no other. Every step could be her last. Every breath might be her final one.

Of course, she'd been in this place before. Of wondering if she would make it or if the next moment would be her last.

Mina reached the pathway and gave in to the desire to look back once.

Webster still stood where she had left him. He nodded once. The gun was in his holster, his hands behind his back.

Mina walked on as fast as she could with her injuries. The path felt like it went for miles, but she made it to the kitchen door and shut it behind her, leaning against it to take in a deep breath. Then she continued on, making it to her car. She set the satchel in the passenger seat and only then considered what she could do with the money: pay off her medical bills.

Before taking off, she sent a text to her contact at the temp agency.

I quit.

Safe Inside

Violet ran from the house, shoving her phone into her pocket. Her stepdad called out behind her, "Violet, get back here now and take your punishment." Like anyone would turn back at those words. Mark was a bastard, drunk and violent. Her mom was a useless bitch who let him do whatever he wanted to both of them. Not today. Violet was through taking his abuse. She was never going back. Mom had made her choice.

The air cooled as Violet entered the forest. The dimming of the sunshine calmed her, made her feel less overwhelmed. The smells in here were rich and pleasant, clean. Not like the odors in the house of cigarettes, cheap beer, grease, and armpit sweat. Daddy Mark, as he made Violet call him, was unclean in addition to being a terrible person. His hair was so oily it stayed however it landed if he ran his hands through it, and there were such intense armpit stains on his shirts that her mom couldn't get them out, so they just compounded, darkening.

The soft crunch of damp twigs beneath her feet soothed Violet, and she slowed her steps, taking in the trees and plant life. Ferns had always been her favorite. There were blackberry bushes on the edge of the forest, too, but she'd already rushed past those. They liked to get a little sun, and often grew along the roads back here in the rural area. Mom always told her not to eat berries from the roadside bushes, because they'd have motor oil and stuff like that on them, but they tasted fine to

Violet every time she popped one into her mouth. They couldn't be that bad.

It was easy to keep walking in here, to wander and let her feet take her wherever they wanted. Where the sun broke through the foliage, it created lace patterns that speckled the ground and surrounding trunks. Occasionally, a breeze rustled through the leaves and sent the light swirling. She tried to shut off thoughts of Mom and Daddy Mark, of the fact that there was no escaping for her now. It was easy enough to tell herself that she could leave and find a better life, but at only fifteen that wasn't a viable option unless she could come up with a plan. There was the matter of where to go, how to get money for food and someplace to live. And who knew what else. She didn't know what it took to live on her own.

She couldn't keep living in that house, though. With those people.

Maybe finding her dad was an option. She'd tried searching online before, but there had to be a better way.

A massive tree rose before Violet, its top branches lost above the forest canopy. All the other trees were several feet away, making a ring of sorts that faded away into the forest. Leaves in varying states of decay littered the surrounding ground. Some were green and soft, while others were brown and crisp. She walked through them, enjoying the crunch of the dry leaves beneath her feet. The closer she got, the larger the tree seemed. Its gnarled trunk showcased thick, rutted bark. Moss grew along the roots and lower trunk.

Violet placed a hand on the trunk, feeling the roughness under her fingers. She turned and sat on the firm ground, back against the tree, legs crossed. The scratch of the bark felt real. It grounded her. Closing her eyes, she lay her head back against the tree and took a deep breath, holding it in.

A loud creak sounded.

She opened her eyes.

There was nothing visible other than the trees. It must have been one of them. She closed her eyes again, trying to relax. Deep breath in through the nose, hold. She blew the air out through her mouth, slow, deliberate. There'd been a section of gym on yoga, and this breathing was one thing she'd retained from it. Several more times, and she worked to clear her mind, to cut out thoughts of what Daddy Mark did to her, of her mother's eyes that showed she knew exactly what her boyfriend did to her daughter, of the smells and sensations of the crappy mobile home. Each time she cleared her mind, thoughts popped back in unbidden.

A montage occurred in her mind. Daddy Mark giving her "the look," the one that told her he'd be by later, that he was appraising her and thinking about what he wanted to do. Mom's eyes sparkling with unshed tears just before she turned her back on Violet. The constant arguments. The feeling of hunger when Daddy Mark and Mom didn't feel like going grocery shopping, so they took off together for hours at a time, leaving Violet behind to eat crackers with ketchup on them. The sound of the door creaking open, slow and dread-inducing.

Something creaked again, this time longer.

Violet's eyes opened. She looked around, taking in the shadows and the dancing lights. Then she looked up, up, up, into the tree's higher branches. It looked slightly crooked now, as if the trunk had bent partway up.

A crack came from her right, as if someone had stepped on a branch. She startled and looked in that direction.

Nothing.

Now from her left, a similar sound, joined by the crunch of leaves.

Nothing in that direction either.

Having the tree at her back made her feel safe from that direction, but she felt otherwise exposed out here, far away from anyone who could hear her scream. How far had Violet walked before she found this tree? She'd never seen it before, not in years of walking into the woods, so it had to be farther than usual.

Was she lost?

There was no sign of a distinctive path to tell her where to go. Of course, she was facing the direction from which she'd come, so that would get her started, but after that she didn't remember having followed a path. She'd just walked, lost in her thoughts, determined to move forward. Or move away. She'd wanted to escape the house and the people in it, so she'd wandered for however long without really paying attention. There hadn't been many impediments, so it made sense that there had been a path she'd followed subconsciously.

A rustling came, growing nearer.

Violet stood up, back still against the tree, palms flat against the bark. She tried to determine where the sounds came from, but they bounced off the trees, sending out false directional signals.

The rustling stopped.

Straining her eyes in the sun-dappled dimness of the forest, Violet looked for anything that might explain the noise. There should have been wildlife here. There should have been bugs. There were always bugs. If there were any here right now, they were good at staying hidden, maybe working industriously underneath the leaves or burrowing under the bark.

That was not the rustling she'd heard, though. Nor were bugs responsible for the creaking and cracking. The noises were too big, too loud. Something larger lurked in the woods.

Violet took a step forward. She felt the loss of the tree's stability against her back, a void of sensation.

The rustling started once more, but this time it didn't stop. She glimpsed a discreet shifting of the leaves in a swerving line that headed in her direction. It looked like something was burrowing forward underneath the leaves. They shifted and slid down from a slightly raised hump.

It moved toward her.

Unsure of what to do to evade whatever moved underneath the leaves, Violet turned and tried to climb the tree. It loomed so large that she couldn't get her arms around the trunk, not even around to the sides. The tree was as wide as she was tall.

She tried to find handholds or footholds in the bark. Anything that might facilitate a safe escape up the trunk. There were some furrows wide enough for her fingers, but when she clamped her hands around the bark, it broke off in her hand, soggy. It rained here quite a bit, and the tree seemed to hold water beneath the surface. The last storm had been days ago, yet here was the moisture to prove the tree had retained the water.

A skittering over the leaves drew her attention.

When she turned around, the skittering stopped. Nothing moved. Even the thing under the leaves had ceased.

She turned back to the tree and tried to wedge her fingers into the bark, but too much of it crumbled away. Instead, she tried to jump toward the lowest branch. She missed.

Another jump. The tips of her fingers grazed the branch.

The skittering started again. So did the rustle of the thing beneath the leaves.

She didn't want to look. But she had to.

Turning to look netted her only stillness. A couple leaves shifted slightly as if there had just been motion nearby and they hadn't yet settled.

Another jump, and the fingers of one hand hooked over the branch. It was just enough to hang there for a split second before her hand slid off.

The skittering was more persistent this time, louder, closer, more frantic.

She turned, pressing her back to the tree.

Where there had been bare ground in the circle around the big tree, there were now a multitude of trees. These were slimmer, obviously younger, their bark not as deep and rutted. Their roots stretched out above the ground as if they had just stopped on the surface. As she looked, one root shot outward and dove beneath the leaves, joining the rustling of another one already under the ground cover.

More of the roots dove or slid forward, disappearing beneath the leaves.

Something wrapped around her ankle and yanked. It burned her, pain shooting up her leg in the seconds it took to fall face forward. A sharp pain jolted up into her gums and she tasted blood. It filled her mouth, even after she spit it onto the ground.

Rolling onto her back, Violet reached for her ankle. Her fingers met bark, thinner than that on the large tree, finer furrows and ridges than on the trunk.

It was one of the roots, rough, but not as rough as the tree's bark.

The swish of leaves came from her side.

Violet wrestled with the thing wrapped around her ankle,

trying to yank herself free. She curled her fingers around it and tried to wedge them underneath so she could break it, but it was too tight. It cut into her skin.

Another root wrapped around her arm just above the elbow and pulled at her.

Every time she blinked or looked away, the trees shifted. They were getting closer.

"Violet!" came the smoke-roughened voice of Daddy Mark. "Get your ass home." He sounded far away, but if he'd made it this far, there was a chance he'd find her.

As she rested there on the ground, the scent of decay from beneath the leaves strong in her nose, roots tightening on her ankle and arm, others worming their way toward her under the leaves, Violet thought about the escape she'd hoped to make. How badly she wanted to be anywhere but home. That place called home, anyway, which was nothing like it was supposed to be. There was nothing there for her. All she'd ever wanted in life was someone to love her and treat her like she mattered.

She placed a hand against the giant tree's trunk. Her fingers sunk into the bark with a slight resistance, almost as of set gelatin.

The trunk quivered.

Her hand felt warm, cocooned...safe.

She pushed her hand deeper into the tree. Resistance ceased.

More roots wrapped around her torso, her arms and legs. One wrapped around her throat and squeezed. It felt rough and tight, the friction burning her skin and leaving it raw.

It cut her air off. She struggled to draw a breath.

Her arm wasn't only sinking now—something pulled at it, bringing her body closer to the giant tree. She was elbow deep now.

Branches swooped down and beat at the trees. Roots burst from the soil and leaves, missing Violet, but attaching themselves to the slim roots imprisoning her. These roots were bigger, stronger. They tore at the ones that hurt her.

The smaller roots snapped. Those remaining let go and shot back under the leaves.

The branch she'd been trying to grasp reached down and

cradled Violet in a hard embrace. It lifted her slowly to her feet, the arm inside the trunk moving through it like it would through water.

"Violet, where are you, you useless little brat?" He'd gotten closer.

Another branch came down. Both branches hugged her, pulling her in closer to the trunk.

Violet put her other hand against the bark and watched this time as it sunk in like the first had. She lifted a foot and stepped inside, hitting that mild resistance at first, then getting through it.

She took a deep breath and pressed her face to the bark. It let her through. At first it felt like she couldn't push forward as she had done with her hands, but then she got through that layer of resistance and found her entire body inside the tree. It wasn't hollow. In fact, there was a substance all around that pressed against her with warmth and support. It coated her skin like a film, yet she could breathe through it. There was oxygen here.

Daddy Mark's voice was muffled when he called her name again.

His scream, when it followed, was muffled, too.

Violet curled into a ball and fell asleep to the sound of Daddy Mark's final shrieks of pain and terror.

The trees took their time.

Such a Good Sleeper

Trigger Warning: See p.116 for details – warning: spoilers

Janelle checked on the baby one more time before the guests arrived. He was fast asleep, swaddled in a mint-green blanket. So still. So peaceful. As a single mother to a newborn there were times where the stress of it got to her, made her question her choices and abilities as a mom, but then moments like this came along. She stroked a finger along his silky cheek then backed out of the room, careful to keep the knob turned as the door shut so there would be no click to wake him up.

Out front, car doors shut. She peeked out the window and saw they'd arrived. No need for loud knocks or a ringing doorbell to wake the baby, she opened the door and waited for them to stroll up the sidewalk. Mandy carried a casserole dish covered in aluminum foil. People had been incredibly nice about bringing food to Janelle since the birth. In fact, there'd been so much food delivered in such large quantities that things she couldn't freeze had gone in the garbage. She simply couldn't eat it all. Maybe if there'd been a man of the house they could have made a dent, but a single mom didn't need this much food.

Mandy and Scott got up to the porch. After handing the dish off to Scott, Mandy threw her arms around Janelle. "Happy

Mother's Day!"

Janelle returned the hug. "Thank you. And thank you both for coming over. It felt weird to be alone today."

"Of course," Mandy said. "We're always up for dinner with a friend. The kids were excited to get both Mother's Day and Grandmother's Day."

"Come on in." Janelle stepped inside and gestured. She couldn't help comparing her outfit to Mandy's. Here was Mandy, wearing a cute little dress with a denim jacket, looking slim and fresh, cheeks pink, hair pulled back in a slick ponytail. Meanwhile, Janelle wore a pair of sweatpants that hadn't been washed in an unknown period of time, an oversized shirt with stains on it, and her hair was pulled back in a sloppy semi-bun held by a claw clip. She hadn't so much as looked at makeup since little Eric had been born two weeks ago, or probably for a couple months before that, and Mandy had on exactly the right amount for that "natural" look that wasn't natural at all and had probably taken her thirty minutes to do, at least. There was nothing glamorous about single motherhood.

"Where's Eric?" Scott asked.

"He's napping. Such a good sleeper! I got lucky."

"Is he already sleeping through the night?" Mandy asked as she walked to the stove. "Are you okay with me sticking this in the oven to heat up?"

"Yep, go ahead. And yes, he sleeps through the night. Has been for the last week. That first morning I woke up and found sun streaming in the window instead of the usual darkness, it was glorious."

"I bet," said Scott.

"He never cries, either. Not since that first week. I don't know how I got so lucky with such a good baby, but I'm going to enjoy it while it lasts."

"Oh man, I swear Monica didn't sleep through the night until she was about ten months old," Mandy said. "She probably cried enough for both her and Eric, so you're welcome." She laughed. "I took that hit so you didn't have to."

"I figure it's the least fate or karma or whatever it is could do after stealing his father away from me."

Silence greeted this pronouncement. Instantly, Janelle felt

bad for going there and bringing down the mood. It had been months since Barclay's death, time enough to grieve what was an early relationship to begin with. The shocking news of her pregnancy had come about a week after he'd died. They'd had sex once. One time, a first for her to climb into bed with someone on the first date. He'd been so attractive, with dark skin, and light eyes, but that hadn't been enough. It had been how much he'd seemed to understand her, his charm, his ability to listen and know exactly what she was trying to say.

Then he was gone. She thought he'd ghosted her, but then a family member had contacted her in response to a text she'd sent him and let her know that he'd been taken suddenly by a heart attack. He was only thirty-two, much too young to die of a heart attack. They said it was an undiagnosed condition, a ticking time bomb, and that he'd been lucky to grow past infancy to begin with.

Knowing she faced raising a child with no financial support, Janelle had considered every option, but she'd wanted this baby. She had a good job, flexibility to work from home, and decent maternity leave. Plus, she had supportive friends, like the two sitting in this room, looking anywhere but at her, because she'd made it awkward.

Saved by the baby, a gurgle sounded from his room.

"He's awake! I'll be back in a minute, and you can finally meet him." She hurried from the room, heartened by the delighted gasp Mandy let out.

Eric lay in his crib, calm, little airy sounds coming from his mouth along with bubbles. He was wet when she picked him up, his diaper full to overflowing, pajamas soaked, so she set about changing his diaper, wiping him down with baby-powder-scented wipes, and putting new footie pajamas on. "Did you get all hot and sweaty?" His skin felt clammy to the touch. The unseasonably warm weather had heated the house.

He looked up at her. She felt the warmth of his love and of hers in return. Not once had she felt like this had been a mistake.

Scooping him up into her arms, careful to hold his head, which still felt damp, she took him out to the living room. "Say hi to your Aunt Mandy and Uncle Scott." She held him up so they could see his precious face. One hand cradled his head, the other his diapered butt. He felt so soft and delicate and small, a fragile being. It struck her in that moment how much he depended on her, the odd power being a mother granted her. It was terrifying and awe-inspiring at the same time. She knew in that moment she would always keep him safe.

Janelle brought him in close again, snuggling him to her chest. She felt her own heart beating where his cheek lay.

When she looked up, she couldn't decipher the look on Mandy's face. Her friend's expression was almost frightened. A ball of hurt confusion formed in Janelle's stomach. "Why are you looking at me like that? Why are you looking at Eric that way?"

"Is this a joke, Janelle?" Mandy asked.

Her words stung. They didn't make sense. Janelle looked down at her baby boy. She'd missed something. Maybe his pajamas were on wrong. She looked for a tear or a misplaced button, but everything was where it should be. Self-consciously, she brushed a hand over his fine hair and smoothed it into place.

Scott took the three steps to bring him next to Mandy. He wrapped his arm around her and pulled her close to him. "Where's the baby?"

They were playing a prank. Had to be. Relief flooded through Janelle, loosening the ball in her stomach. "Very funny, you guys." She tried to let out a small laugh, but it came out more a nervous choking than a genuine laugh. This prank felt cruel. Hurt still throbbed inside her from

their reactions. They were the first ones to see Eric, to bother coming to visit. Her own parents kept making excuses for why they couldn't come see their grandchild. Their archaic opinions against a child out of wedlock were more important than Janelle and Eric.

This was not at all what she'd been expecting.

Scott released Mandy and stalked toward Janelle. She pulled the baby in tight and shifted her body to protect him.

Scott brushed past her with more force than she'd expected, and she stumbled, keeping a tight hold on Eric. She turned as Scott walked into Eric's bedroom, disappearing from sight. The sound of items being moved—scuffing, the padded clunk of wood on carpet, something scratching along the wall—came from the room. The metallic *sproing* of the crib's bottom echoed.

Out came Scott, holding what looked like the sheet from the crib mattress. Some sort of greenish-black substance had stained it. "I don't know what you're trying to pull. Where's the baby? What is all over this sheet?"

Confused, Janelle looked down at Eric again. They were acting like they couldn't see him. If this was a joke, they'd taken it too far. "I want you both out. Now."

"Listen—"

Mandy held up a hand, stopping Scott. She brought that hand back to her chest where the other one already clenched and wrapped them together. Taking a couple steps toward Janelle, she stopped as if she'd hit a wall. "Janelle, honey, what's that smell?"

"Excuse me?"

"Can't you smell that?"

Janelle resisted lifting Eric up to smell his diaper. She'd just changed it. What a ridiculous question. Unless Mandy's sense of smell was so keen she could smell the dirty diaper in the bedroom. Instead, she pressed her lips together and stared back at Mandy. "I asked you to leave."

Mandy's eyes teared up. Something changed in her face, a tightening of the features. She reached out a hand, but Janelle jerked away and stepped back. Mandy pulled her own arm back in response. "I'm sorry, Janelle. Can I see him?" Her voice was oddly soft.

Janelle felt like she was being handled, like they thought she was crazy. But she couldn't figure out why. She'd been friends with Mandy for at least twenty years, and she looked genuinely worried. Mandy had never been able to keep herself from giggling when she was pranking someone. Certainly she'd never been able to fake tears. It had been Janelle who could do that. Not only that, but waves of physical anger came off Scott. They battered Janelle's back, her raw senses tuned in to any movement coming from behind her in case he came at her again.

"Why would I let you anywhere near him when you're acting like this?" Janelle asked. Their behavior was bizarre. She didn't feel safe, didn't feel Eric was safe with these people here.

Crazy thoughts spun through her head. They were trying to take him. They didn't feel she was a fit mother, so they were gaslighting her. The eeriness of their combined behavior had her on the verge of believing in possession.

Eric had behaved so far, but he had to be getting hungry. Janelle willed him to stay peaceful a little longer, in case his cries would further trigger Scott and Mandy. She needed to do whatever it took to get them out and lock the door behind them. They had no right to judge her or her son.

She'd thought they'd love Eric. She was going to ask them to be his godparents. It had been days of nervous planning, figuring they'd be more likely to say yes if they were holding him when Janelle asked. There had even been rehearsals in the mirror to get it just right. They already had kids of their own. Mandy was her most trusted friend, making it only natural that they be the designated guardians if anything happened to Janelle, to ensure Eric would be cared for by people who would love him like their own.

Maybe they wanted him too much already.

Scott moved behind her, a shuffling, a shifting of air, and Janelle sidestepped, twisting just enough so she could keep both of them in her sight. "I won't tell you again. Get out of my house." She kept her voice firm, amazed that it didn't shake.

The rage was still naked across Scott's face, but his eyes squinted now in puzzlement. "You're not joking, are you?"

Mandy's voice was sharp. "Scott." A whiplash of sound. "Be quiet."

Janelle looked around for an exit or a weapon. If she could get to the front door, which stood behind Mandy, she could run to a neighbor's house. Surely they'd let her in when they saw Eric in her arms. At the very least, there'd be witnesses if anything happened outside. Someone might hear her screaming for help.

She backed up until her legs pressed against the sofa. It helped her feel rooted, as if at least her back was protected.

Without taking her eyes off the people she'd mistook for

friends, she moved sideways, careful of the glass coffee table that she'd already wrapped in cushioning to hide the sharp corners from Eric's soft flesh and brittle young bones. The more distance she had between them, the better.

There had been a heavy glass dish on the end table that now stood directly behind her, but she'd moved that during her babyproofing, too. Anything dangerous had been socked away in the attic. Save picking up the heavy end table, there was nothing she could use as a weapon. The only things that would do damage would require her to put the baby down to pick them up.

She could keep something between her and the two of them. That she could do.

Just as she had been conscious of the difference between the way Mandy looked and the way Janelle looked, Janelle was now painfully aware of how out of shape she'd become during her pregnancy. She still held at least half the weight she'd gained, probably more. It was all soft and fat. She hadn't been a big exerciser before, and she sure wasn't during her pregnancy. Food had been the focus, her hunger overwhelming at times. Scott could certainly overpower her, but realistically, so could Mandy. At least right now.

Janelle had never had to look at her best friend to determine which of them was stronger. They'd been a united force since their teens. It hurt that she had to do so now.

Scott started to come around the back of the sofa, less than a yard of distance between them, rapidly closing the gap she'd tried to create.

Mandy came around the other side of the coffee table, though it didn't seem like she wanted to come too close to Janelle. She kept hesitating, her body leaning backward. It looked like she had to force herself forward. She stopped maybe two feet away and gazed into Janelle's eyes. "What if I make Scott go outside? Will you let me look at Eric?"

"I'm not leaving—"

Mandy looked at him, putting on a strict face Janelle was used to seeing her use around the kids, but rarely on her husband. "If she wants you outside, you go outside."

"I'm not comfortable with either of you near him," Janelle

said. She needed them to leave, and she needed to call the police to report an attempted kidnapping.

"I'm just a little worried, Janelle. Eric looks like he might be sick. It happens with newborns. They've been in a bubble for months, and then they come out and get exposed to all the germs in the hospital. I want to make sure he's okay, and then I'll leave."

He wasn't sick. He was perfect. This was just Mandy trying to get her hands on him.

"I said no."

"Okay, but can I ask you a question?"

"What?" Janelle hit the "T" hard, biting it off.

"Does he hold your finger when you touch his palm?"

"Of course he does."

"Can you try it right now? I promise I'll leave after you do it."

"Why would I humor you?"

Without taking her eyes off Janelle, Mandy said, "Scott, can you go outside and call the kids to make sure they're okay?"

"But—"

"I asked you to go outside and make a call, Scott."

It was odd how Mandy kept using everyone's names. Like she was making a point of it. Janelle realized that if Scott went outside, an entire exit would be opened up to her. She could run out the back door or lock herself in the master bedroom.

Janelle straightened up. "Okay, if Scott leaves I'll try it."

Scott sighed, then gave an angry grunt. "I'll go call the kids, but I'm just going to be outside the door." He looked at Janelle. "Got it?"

Janelle squinted at him. *He* was the one threatening *her*. The two of them had come into her home, and now they were trying to take her infant. He had no right to act like this.

It didn't matter. Anything that got him out of the house was worth it.

"Got it."

There was a phone in her room. All she needed was to get back there and shut the door. She needed to solidify her plan, not just blindly run and make choices as she went.

His location meant he'd have to cross that opening between

the sofa and the table where Janelle had come through. If he ran at her, she'd have to be able to get away.

She took two large steps backwards. This took her past the end table to a small open area between it and the wall. She could run behind the sofa and get it between them again.

Realizing she had tensed her arms and was squeezing Eric, Janelle consciously relaxed her grip on his small form. He hadn't moved, hadn't made a sound. She glanced down quick enough to verify he was okay.

He looked fine.

Scott moved to the end of the sofa. He stared at her, shifted his body to face her. His body tensed.

Janelle stepped sideways until she was behind the arm of the sofa. She looked at the distance to the hallway that led back to the bedrooms.

It looked so far away. So much distance to cover.

She could do it if she needed to. What about that super mom strength women had when their children were in danger? She could sprint, plow forward, make it to the bedroom and the phone. Anything to keep Eric safe.

Scott grunted again, turned, and strode to the front door, footsteps heavy. He opened it and stepped outside, closing the door behind him.

Part of Janelle wanted to relax at his absence, but she knew she needed to be ready to run. She tensed her legs and torso in preparation.

"Janelle..."

"Stop saying my name...*Mandy*."

"Okay, I'm sorry." Mandy sat down in the easy chair facing and parallel to the coffee table and sofa. "I'm not coming after you. Can you check that one thing for me? Maybe he's just dehydrated. You know how often they have to eat at this age. Of course you do. You're his mother."

"Exactly. Which is how I know he's okay."

"Sometimes there aren't any clear signs until they're really sick."

Janelle started toward the hallway. There was no reason to keep talking to Mandy now.

"Wait!" Mandy's voice broke.

Janelle stopped.

"Please, I'm begging you. I care about you and Eric." Mandy's words came fast. "I'm sorry we were acting weird. He just looked dehydrated. We should have let you feed him, and I'm sure it would have been fine."

They looked at each other.

Mandy remained in the chair, relaxing back into it. "I overreacted. It's been a long time since I was around a baby. Monica's eight, you know. It's been forever since she was Eric's age."

Janelle struggled against her inclination to trust Mandy. The way Scott had acted had nothing to do with mild concern. He'd looked to be on the verge of violence. She'd never seen him that angry.

"Will you sit down? We can talk."

Every fiber of Janelle's being wanted to sit down and let things be normal again, to talk to her best friend and let her hold Eric, to hear her coo like Janelle had done over Mandy's babies. Things had gone so wrong. She'd imagined how it would be, how beautiful they'd find Eric. She'd known they would fall in love with him instantly the way she had.

Mandy had been there for her so many times. It didn't make sense that she would turn on Janelle now. Besides, Mandy had said she didn't want more kids, that two was enough. Maybe Janelle needed to show how okay Eric was and Mandy would leave her alone.

Easing back around the sofa, Janelle sat down, leaning on the arm. She didn't sit all the way back, ready to spring up if needed. No matter what was going on, Eric needed to eat. It had been hours since he last nursed. She lifted her shirt, unclasped the nursing bra flap, and eased Eric onto her nipple. They'd told her it would get easier to nurse as time went on, and it had. She didn't even feel it anymore, really, just the dampness of his mouth. There was no longer the sensation of her milk letting down, that weird rush of feeling in the milk ducts.

A choking sound came from Mandy's direction, but when Janelle looked up, her friend was still seated, face blank.

Janelle picked up his tiny hand and wrapped it in hers. He felt cool to the touch, no longer hot from his nap.

They sat in silence for a while. So much for talking, but Janelle actually preferred this. Once Eric had his fill, they'd be able to talk. He'd probably go right back to sleep.

Mandy kept looking toward the door. This time, when she looked back, Janelle made a point of staring at her. Their eyes met, and Mandy smiled. It didn't reach her eyes, and she looked nervous, biting her bottom lip, blinking a lot. It was a good reminder that the situation wasn't back to normal, that there was still danger lurking here.

I'll feed him, and then I'll say I need to change his diaper.

Several minutes passed without anything being said. Then Mandy's phone chimed. She picked up the phone and looked at the screen, relief quickly showing itself in the relaxing of her face and shoulders. When she looked up and saw Janelle watching her, a wave of some emotion scrolled over her face before it blanked out again. Guilt, maybe. "That was my mom, just letting me know the kids were behaving."

Eric appeared to have fallen asleep again. Janelle extracted her nipple and reconnected the bra flap. It hadn't taken long for her to get good at doing it with one hand. "Okay, you wanted to talk. You can see he's fine. He's nursed. What's the issue?"

"Can I hold him?"

"The answer's still no."

"Okay. Can I ask when he started sleeping through the night?"

Janelle let out a frustrated huff. "I already told you. A week. Well, six days, but that's long enough for me to know it's a trend, not an outlier."

A fly landed on Eric's face, and she batted it away without touching him. The flies had been constant all week, spring in full bloom.

"When did his belly become so bloated?"

Janelle frowned. "Now you're criticizing his body? Baby's have round stomachs. You should know that."

Mandy pressed her lips together.

Janelle had had enough. "You know, I trusted you. I thought you'd come here and be so happy to see him, that you'd want to love on him. Instead, all you've done is insult both of us. Are you jealous? You've had your kids. It's my turn now. And,

65

frankly, I expected more support from you."

Mandy started to cry, this time the tears leaking from her eyes and flowing down her cheeks. "I know." She bit her lip again, looked at the door.

"Stop looking at the door!"

Mandy snapped her eyes back to Janelle's.

Mandy's phone chimed again.

The doorknob turned.

Janelle stood up, pressing Eric to her chest.

The door started to open, a slow, measured movement.

Janelle moved around the sofa, putting it between her and the door. Scott was not going to come near her again.

Someone stepped inside. A man, but it wasn't Scott.

It took Janelle a moment to recognize the police uniform. Another officer stepped in behind the first. They looked at her and spread out, the male cop moving toward the hallway, efficiently blocking her escape. The other took several steps until she was nearly at the sofa. The woman's face remained blank, just as Mandy's had been, though her eyes flitted toward the baby and away repeatedly. The male cop held a hand to his stomach, his skin a sick, pale color that was almost green.

Another woman entered, this one in a suit instead of a uniform. She looked around the room, spotted Janelle, and moved next to the officer nearest the couch. "Janelle?" she asked.

Janelle didn't answer. She didn't understand what was happening. Had Scott told them she'd done something to him?

The woman in the suit cleared her throat. "Janelle, my name is Rebecca Lathrop. I'm a social worker. Your friend called in a concern about your wellbeing and the health of your son." She broke eye contact long enough to look down at the baby.

"He's not my friend," Janelle said of Scott, knowing it must have been him who called.

"Janelle, was Eric...it is Eric, correct?"

"Yes."

"Okay, has Eric been acting out of the ordinary at all?"

"He's two weeks old. There is no ordinary yet."

"That's fair. Have you seen any behaviors that made you nervous or unsure?"

"No, he's perfect."

Rebecca moved until she was directly across from Janelle, the sofa between them. "I need you to hand me your son so I can check him out."

Janelle took a step back. The cop by the hallway pulled his weapon at the same time as the one near the sofa took two rapid steps forward and held out a hand.

Janelle froze.

This was unreal. Did Scott and Mandy know what harm they were doing? People already looked down on single mothers. She'd done nothing wrong. They were going to make her lose her child. None of this judgmental attitude had shown during her pregnancy. In fact, they'd very much seemed to be there for her, making sure she ate, doing grocery runs for her when she'd gotten too busy wrapping up loose ends at work, accompanying her to doctor's appointments.

"He'll be safe with me, Janelle. I just need to check on him."

Seeing no choice, Janelle stretched her arms out, handing him over to Rebecca. The woman knelt down in front of the sofa and set Eric on one of the cushions. She bent his arm up, placing his hand by his ear, then pressed her fingers to the inside of his arm about midway between the shoulder and the elbow.

She shot a look over to the female cop and shook her head.

Then she stood up and left Eric on the sofa.

"He could roll off," Janelle said, bending over to reach for her son.

Rebecca held out her hand, "No. I need you to stay on that side of the sofa and leave him be."

"He's my baby."

"Janelle, when did Eric die?"

It felt like she'd been belted. Janelle shook her head. "What are you talking about?" Was everyone crazy? "He's fine."

"I'm no medical examiner, but this baby has clearly been dead for several days. His stomach is bloated, though it's going down now. There's fluid leaking from under his eyelids and out of his nose. His tongue is still slightly bloated. His skin is *green*. Surely you have to be able to see that." Now Rebecca's voice shook.

Everyone stared at Janelle. They all looked sick and angry

and disgusted. They were looking at her like she was a pile of shit. The male officer hadn't put away his weapon. His lips pulled back from his teeth.

Janelle looked down at Eric once more.

At first he looked perfect, with sand-colored skin and blond curls.

The more she looked, the more that changed. His skin had darkened to a deep green in places and he looked damp, shiny with fluids. His hair was limp, clumps of it missing. His pajamas were stained with dark fluids. A patch of skin was missing from his cheek.

He looked waxy. His hands were limp. Glazed eyes stared straight ahead.

That's when the smell hit her. Decay, rotten meat, feces.

And she remembered. Remembered going to his bedroom that morning she'd slept in so late, not having been woken up. Remembered finding him unresponsive, stiff. Remembered clutching his small body to hers, feeling it cool as she held him.

Remembered finding her baby boy dead at just a week old.

Then it was like her mind had blanked it all out, made her see him as whole and alive. Perfect. For days now she had toted around his corpse, changed his diapers which were full of body fluids, changed his clothes to get rid of the stained cotton, stuck his cool mouth on her nipple as if he were feeding. She'd dried out, no more milk being produced, but as the memories flashed back she remembered the pain of her engorged breasts when he wasn't suckling from them anymore, even before that day, the leakage onto her shirts and bras. She looked down and saw the stains, from both her milk and his body.

She threw herself over the back of the sofa, pulling him to her, holding his limp body, and she sobbed for the first time since finding him dead. Her body shook with her grief, stomach hitching. She yelled, guttural, so loud that it tore up her throat coming out.

This went on for some time before she got up, wiped the tears from her face, smiled, and asked, "Does anyone want to hold Eric? He's such a good sleeper, it won't even wake him up."

Of Wicker and Mead

Christy watched the festivities through the bars of her cell window. It was a small jail, and she was the only person there. The jailer had brought her some sort of sausage and bread earlier. He'd been dressed in a green robe or dress with designs around the bottom. He'd worn something that looked like a tiara made of leaves. He was out there now, celebrating Beltane with the rest of the town.

A lot of people were dressed up in costumes that ranged from elf-looking to historical, maybe medieval. It was bright and crazy, and everyone ran around laughing and shouting. It would have been fun to be out there joining in the revelry, but instead Christy sat in a prison, accused of something she hadn't done. They'd told her the magistrate would be off for several more days, and to get used to the maybe ten-by-ten cell. She'd never even heard of Beltane, yet here she was, locked up because someone had broken the branch off a tree, and she'd happened to see it and pick it up.

The premise was absurd to begin with. A broken branch didn't seem like a horrible offense. They'd said something about the "little people" and a bunch of Gaelic she couldn't quite wrap her brain around. They'd repeated something that sounded like "Ees-she." Her protests had fallen on deaf ears, as well. Likely, the fact that she was a tourist hadn't helped. She hadn't intended to even stop in this town, but she'd seen some sort of butterfly and followed it off the road. It had been a huge bug, with colorful wings like nothing she'd ever seen before. They'd been multiple shades of greens, blues, and purples, and they swirled instead of there being dots and wavy lines. It was almost a tie-dye.

It had disappeared into the tree. That's when she'd seen the branch lying there and picked it up. The branch had major spikes on it. They must have been two or three inches long. Vaguely, she remembered this must be a hawthorn. She was going to use it to move the branches aside so she could see through the foliage and find the butterfly, not to touch it, but just to get a closer look and maybe a cell phone picture.

The guy had appeared out of nowhere. Somewhere out of sight, anyway. He was tall and wiry, blond, with patches of hair on his cheeks and chin that hadn't formed a cohesive beard. He'd grabbed her, and despite trying to fight him off, his fingers had been like steel. None of her landed hits had fazed him.

They'd gone up a hill, and there, below, had been the town. The surrounding hills were green, and the town had done its best to blend in with greens and browns on the buildings and copious shrubs and plants. People stared as he marched her past them, no one helping when she told them this man had kidnapped her.

He'd brought her here.

It could have been worse.

They'd taken her phone away, so her only entertainment was to watch folks getting inebriated, eating, and playing various games. There was dancing, too, and a giant pole they'd wrapped some sort of streamers or ribbons around. That, she was at least familiar with. She knew it as a May Pole, but they'd called it something else.

The sun was starting to dip, and several men disappeared for a few minutes, coming back with barrels they rolled across the ground and set in a large, rough circle. Next, young boys ran off, calling to each other in high, eager voices. When they came back, the sun sat just above the horizon. Their arms were full of sticks and small logs. These went into the barrels. As the boys dispersed, a woman lit a large torch and stood in the center of the circle. Other women joined her with torches of their own, all lighting them from the original torch. They used these to light the wood in the barrels, and fire sprung up, brightening the surroundings even as the sun disappeared entirely, flinging its one final light show up behind it that faded to midnight blue.

Now little girls danced around the barrels, skirts swirling, ribbon-twined hair flying. Their giggles turned into sweet songs. Mugs and glasses made their way around the crowd, filled with liquids Christy couldn't see, but from the raucousness of the voices and the dancing she saw, they were clearly full of alcohol.

A woman pointed Christy's way and spoke to a clump of teenage girls, all bedecked with flowers, vines, and long dresses. They looked over, too, then ran toward the jail. They were out of sight for a moment, but the sounds of their footsteps padding across the floor told her they had, indeed, entered the jail. It had seemed like the building had multiple purposes, so maybe they were coming to get something for the festival.

Instead, one rosy-cheeked young woman appeared at the barred entrance to the cell, out of breath, her cheeks pinked from running around in the cooling night. She held the jailer's key ring, which was small, only holding three keys. It appeared there were only two cells total in here, so maybe the extra one was for the front door.

As the girl unlocked the door, the others joined her. There were seven in all, and they were giddy. Several of them held swatches of fabric, flowers, and some sort of vines or twine. They spoke English, heavily flavored with an Irish lilt. A girl who appeared to be the oldest—she was the tallest, anyway—stepped forward. "We're here to prepare you for the festival."

"I get to attend?"

They giggled and looked at each other before the oldest spoke again. "Of course! It can't happen without our esteemed guest."

Christy looked around her cell and gestured at her surroundings. "Odd way to treat an esteemed guest."

A shorter girl with fiery red hair spoke now. "Don't worry. It will all be made right this evening."

They swarmed her, hands and fabric flying. The fabric was actually a dress that resembled some of the ones she'd thought of as historical. It was white, long and flowing, and the sleeves were triangular, getting longer the further they got from her body. The points of the sleeves touched the ground when she held her arms out to the side. A green belt was next, wrapped around her middle, and a rubicund girl with sparkling green eyes said, "Bend forward a little."

When Christy did so, the girl placed a crown of thorns and flowers atop her head. The thorns looked just like the ones from the tree. How were they allowed to pull the thorns off if it was against the law to harm the tree? The flowers smelled strong and sickly sweet. As the smell mingled with the flowers the girls wore, it overwhelmed Christy, and she grew dizzy. The girls still surrounded her, their voices all sounding at the same time. They were in perpetual motion, swirling around her, touching here and there, fixing her hair, and they repeatedly touched her abdomen.

One girl stopped in front of Christy and reached forward, placing her palm flat on Christy's abdomen. She gasped and covered her mouth with the other hand, giggling. Then she took the hand off Christy and brought it to her own abdomen, closing her eyes and breathing deeply. "I can feel it, you guys," she said reverently.

More hands quickly touched Christy's abdomen. With hair and flowers and fabric and leaves and faces a cacophony of motion, she couldn't see who was touching her. The persistent press of hands didn't cease until a loud clap echoed through the cell. There were gasps, the girls otherwise silent, and they all pulled away, opening the space between Christy and a lovely older woman with flowing, white hair, flowers entwined throughout.

The woman pressed her lips together and said, "Out now."

The girls ran from the cell, whispering and laughing, some clasping hands. Christy hadn't realized how tense she was until they were gone. There'd been such youthful exuberance assaulting her with its energy, which had left with the girls, leaving her drained.

"It's nearly time for the ceremony," the woman said. "Come with me and we'll get you some food."

Christy followed her out of the cell and through the small building to the front door. The woman paused at the door, her hand on the knob. She turned to Christy with a small frown wrinkling her brow. "You did come in through this door, right?"

Christy hesitated. "Yes?"

"Good. You must always exit through the same door you entered."

"Great." Which door she'd entered was the last thing on Christy's mind.

They exited the building and turned left to head toward the festivities. A line of people stretched by the jailhouse, each with at least one cow. There hadn't been cattle before, and it caught Christy by surprise. "Where did the cows come from?" she asked.

"Everyone brings their animals for the blessing ritual."

"Is that the ritual I'm doing?"

"No, dear. That one comes later."

The cattle were led between the barrels and away from the celebration. Surprisingly, they were calm about the leaping flames all around them. They walked sedately with their owners, led by ropes, not even paying attention to all the other people around them. They must have been well taken care of. Next, goats were led through in the same way, and reacted similarly to the cattle. Placid, fearless.

Christy was puzzled by her part in all this. One moment she was being accused of breaking a fairy tree or some such bullshit, and the next she wore a dress over her shorts and t-shirt, having to be careful not to trip over her own sleeves. Surely no one had actually worn sleeves like this in the past. They would have died while doing chores. These were completely unrealistic.

Some of the giddiness of the celebration wore off on her, and she couldn't help but feel a bit excited about being in the thick of such celebration.

The woman led Christy to a strange wicker contraption that contained a seat made of twigs. She gestured toward the seat and said, "Here you are. I'll bring you something to eat and drink."

Christy had to step up onto a stone that had been placed in front of the hulking object. She lifted her skirt enough to put one knee up so she could climb into the apparatus. It was almost like a throne of branches, with more to it than that. The apparatus stretched out behind the seat in an odd, bulky way. The seat, once she'd climbed up, wasn't the most comfortable, but it was probably better than sitting on the rock. At least it felt mostly flat, and there weren't any big gaps to make it overly uncomfortable. She settled in the best she could.

Maybe she hadn't really understood what was going on earlier. Perhaps she hadn't even really been arrested. Or they figured it was time served and her fear of being in a foreign prison would be punishment enough for allegedly breaking a branch off a tree. The branch hadn't been clean cut, so it might have fallen off naturally. The guy had overreacted, but maybe he'd calmed down since then. She looked around, trying to spot him in the crowd, but didn't see him anywhere. There were too many people to be able to see much anyway.

The older woman returned, a large plate made of wood in her hand, full of food. The plate was smooth and warm to the touch when Christy took it from her. There was some meat, potatoes with a dollop of butter, sauteed mushrooms, asparagus, and a big piece of bread that had something dark on it.

"Thank you," Christy said. "I haven't asked your name."

The woman handed Christy a mug that smelled like beer, but sweet, and nodded. "It's Maeve."

"Can I ask what all this is? What's the meat?"

"Lamb, oat Bannock, and mead. I imagine you recognize the rest?"

Christy nodded. "Thanks again!"

Maeve walked away, but didn't go far. She gestured for one of the teenage girls to come to her. When the girl did, Maeve leaned in close and spoke into her ear. The girl looked up at Christy, then hastily away when their eyes met. Maeve pulled back, and the girl ran off with the stature of someone with purpose: back straight, arms pumping, chin high.

Christy dug in. The mead was sweet and fruity on her tongue. It tasted of honey. She'd never had lamb, but it wasn't bad. Not her favorite meat, and not one she'd go out of the way for in the future. A bite of everything left her mouth a symphony of flavors, with butter and herbs a lingering taste. She hadn't realized how hungry she was, and the food was quickly consumed, as was the mead. The bread tasted oddly of charcoal. Perhaps it had toppled when they were baking it, and that's what the dark stain had been.

There was nowhere to put the cup and plate, nor could Christy figure out a graceful way down out of the chair. She tried shifting to the side to make room on the seat to at least set down the mug, but there wasn't enough space. Looking around, she tried to meet anyone's gaze to get their attention, but no one looked her way for long. As soon as she felt their gazes meet, the person would look away. Perhaps she truly was a prisoner, and no one wanted anything to do with her. They couldn't possibly think she was dangerous for breaking a branch off a tree.

The bright flicker of flames in the darkness paired with her now full stomach and the mead's effects made her drowsy. She set the mug on the plate and balanced it on her lap, leaning back into the wicker branches that made up the back of the seat. Her eyes drifted shut, but she fought it, jerking them open again. There was so much dancing and vibrancy, and what looked like a lot of flirting. Men held out their arms to women to dance about. Girls primped their hair and fluffed their skirts nervously, studying the boys. Boys laughed and rough housed, eyes drifting over to the girls occasionally to make sure they saw their feats.

Her eyes shut again, the sounds of revelry combining with the pop of burning sap. It diminished to a roar, then faded away.

***

Christy awoke with a start, something cool and wet on her thighs. The mug and plate had fallen from her lap, but not before the remaining mead had spilled. She tried to scratch her nose, but hit resistance against moving her arms. Jerking them did nothing but tighten bonds around her wrists.

She froze.

Rough rope had been tied around her wrists, binding her to the chair. It scratched her skin.

Two of the fires still burned, but there was no one about. Where had everyone gone? And why was she tied up?

Somewhere a child cried.

Someone laughed in the distance.

This time using the bonds to pull herself more upright,

75

Christy peered into the darkness away from the flames, trying to angle her head in such a way as to block out some of the light, which blinded her to the night.

It was no use. She couldn't make out anyone.

Her legs had also been tied to the seat, though they'd had enough give for her to adjust herself. She tugged at her bindings, trying to find a weakness. The more she tugged, the tighter they got. The wood, though strong, flexed. If the ropes wouldn't loosen, maybe the wood would break.

As she worked at her bonds, a sound started. Faint, at first, it grew closer, pounding.

Beyond the fire, something moved. It was fast, heading her way.

A dark shape took flight, leaping through the flames.

Christy jerked backward. Her head slammed into the wooden framework behind her.

A man landed on the ground not far in front of her. He dipped his chin and stared at her for a moment. Firelight flickered in his large, dark pupils. He stood up and moved out of the way just as another shape came from the darkness.

Then they were everywhere, men and teen boys leaping over the fire barrels, criss-crossing as they came over two central barrels, shouting and calling to each other. Raucous laughter bounced between them.

It lasted for several minutes.

Other festival-goers rejoined the fray. They wandered in from the edges of her vision, mugs and glasses raised in a toast. Then they chanted in unison: "Cernunnos, father of the forest, we raise our glasses to you in hopes of your protection for our livestock in the coming months. May our animals be productive, our gardens fruitful, and our loins fertile."

Maeve stepped forward, shadows dancing over her face in the light of the fires. She raised her glass high, everyone else still having theirs up, and called, "Cernunnos, our green man of life, fertility, and death, we ask for your blessing and offer you our sacrifice."

Christy had had enough. This was all quite fascinating, but she wanted to be untied and let go. Barring that, she wanted to go back to the jail to do her time. The wicker branches dug into her butt and thighs, the ropes bit into her wrists and ankles, and she was tired and had the beginnings of a headache. "Excuse me," she called. "Can someone let me out of this?"

No one responded or even looked her way.

The teenage girls from earlier gathered around Maeve. They each held a long stick with fabric wrapped around the end. A pregnant woman approached Maeve with a large bowl the same size as her swollen belly. She looked as if she'd be giving birth any day now.

The woman walked between the girls, who stepped back to allow her through. She handed the bowl, which swayed as if perhaps a liquid were inside, heavy and moving with each step, to the older woman. Maeve took the bowl and gave a deep nod to the woman, who turned and walked away, back through the girls.

The girls created a semi-circle in front of Maeve, their sticks held out. As Maeve looked to each one and gave a shallow nod, the girl plunged the fabric end of her stick into the bowl and brought it out dripping. The strong odor of fermented liquid wafted toward Christy, strong against the smell of wood smoke.

When they had all wetted the end of the stick, the girls split into two groups and walked around Maeve to the fire barrels. They stuck the ends in at the same time, their torches—for that's what they were—bursting into flames.

"Excuse me? I know you can hear me." Christy called. Her pulse throbbed in her throat, face heated. She channeled the rage rushing through her veins and yelled, "Hey!" To no avail. Her throat ached from the guttural yell. She fought her bonds, despite their tightening.

Teenage boys surrounded Christy, working at the wicker pieces surrounding the seat.

Loud foot falls came from the direction of the woods to Christy's left. They vibrated through the seat.

The boys pulled together, lifting more wood tied together with ropes until it surrounded her in a makeshift cage.

Christy fought her bonds, letting them tear into her flesh, relishing the pain because it kept her fighting.

The vibrations increased, the footsteps resounding.

Maeve let out a high-pitched call of some sort and yelled,

"Cernunnos comes!"

Cheers went up.

"Light the wicker man!" Maeve called.

The girls surrounded Christy, their torches bright. Heat radiated out at her, cold spilling in around it, a battle between the two temperatures, both licking at her, tasting her.

Christy didn't know where to look. The light of the flames revealed a pair of eyes, impossibly high in the air, the curve of horns.

The flames caught at the wicker. A flicker at first, then more flickers. Then the flames danced along each bit of wicker, climbing.

A man twice the size of a normal man stepped into view, walking between the two barrels. Despite the reds, oranges, and yellows of the flames, he appeared to be tinted green. His beard hung over his bare chest and reached his waist, flowers braided through it. He had antlers like a deer: branched, curving, and sharp.

Tongues of flame darted at each other, climbing ever higher, circling Christy.

Maeve dropped to her knees before the large man. "We give this sacrifice in your honor. Protect us from the Aos Sì."

"Let me out," screamed Christy.

The binding ropes caught on fire now. Her skin felt as if it were boiling, bubbling...melting.

She pulled the ropes tied around her right wrist taut, straining it. Strands broke loose. The rope unraveled, piece by piece.

Something darted in between the wicker bars. The bug she'd followed earlier.

Only it wasn't a bug. It had a tiny, humanoid body between those large, papery wings.

More of the bugs appeared. They swirled through the bars and around Cernunnos. They attacked the people at the festival.

People ran, screaming, batting at the creatures.

The rope snapped.

Christy's bug, fairy, whatever it was, darted over to her other wrist. She could feel others working at her ankle bindings.

The heat of the fire felt like it was part of her being,

ingrained in her cells.

An ankle broke free.

Cernunnos bugled, a deep, throaty "O" of sound. He turned, racing through those standing around him. The crunch of bones echoed in the air as he stepped on a woman who hadn't moved fast enough. Her screams rose into the sky, only to stop abruptly.

Within seconds, Christy's left hand broke free, followed by the last remaining ankle.

The little, winged people surrounded the cage, unbothered by the flames. They lifted it, freeing Christy from her prison. She jumped down, stumbling after having sat so long, bound.

No one paid her any attention, too busy fleeing the little people.

Biting heat reached her arm, and she realized her sleeve had lit on fire. A towering column of flame shot up the entirety of the sleeve. She tore at it, trying to separate it at the seam. The pain elicited a shriek of agony that burned her throat on the way out.

Then Maeve appeared before her, an iron grip around Christy's other wrist. "You don't know what you're doing, the evil you're freeing."

"The only evil I saw was a village full of people willing to burn a stranger alive." Christy wrenched her wrist free. She brought her flaming arm up and slung it, sending the burning sleeve at Maeve. It whipped around the other woman's neck.

Maeve's hair lit on fire, crumpling and melting, curling upward in clumps. She clawed at the rope of fire around her throat, deep gouges scratching her own face and neck, even as the flesh heated and ran from her skull.

The sleeve tore free of Christy's shoulder. Cold air tip-toed with icy fingers along her damaged skin. She ran, following a group of little people away from the woods, back toward the road.

As she breasted the hill, sobbing reached her ears. She slowed. Up ahead, a man knelt before the hawthorn tree. A wall of little people hovered between him and the tree.

"I didn't mean it." He choked, sobbed. "I didn't mean to break the branch."

Christy came around enough to see his face. It was the blond man who had dragged her into town and accused *her* of breaking the branch.

The green man approached from the woods, his steps rattling the ground. Christy's teeth clacked together. She turned to run, but her tiny savior fluttered in front of her, holding a hand out as if asking her to stay.

Tremors moved through her muscles, her mouth going dry, but she stayed, facing the green man.

Christy's savior flew to the green man, where some sort of nonverbal discussion occurred. The green man grunted, looked toward the kneeling man, and ducked his antlered head. He placed one arm in front of his snout, then brought his head back up.

A flurry of wings batted at the air as a group of little people approached from the party. They carried the domed top portion of the wicker man, still aflame. This, they dropped over the blond man, holding it in place as he screamed and fought to get out.

Christy turned away, sickened by the scent of barbecuing meat and the raw screams.

She still felt this was too harsh a punishment for breaking a branch, but she certainly wasn't going to tell them that. Instead, she held out her palm to the little person who had saved her and waited for them to grasp her finger.

"Thank you."

Then she stepped onto the road and headed back the way she'd come earlier that day.

She didn't know if the screams had stopped, or if she'd just gotten too far away to hear them. Either way, the silence was a relief as she quickly put distance between herself and the town.

Rocket's Red Glare

The explosions sounded at first in a languid string of pops, building in frequency until they were on top of each other, a crescendo of irritation. Even with the curtains closed, the bout of fireworks going off in the street lit the room in brilliant flashes that blinded Emmanuelle. Bones huddled next to her, his ears and tail tucked, quivering at the terrifying concussions.

One more day to Independence Day, yet it had already been a week of this. It came sporadically. She had no way of knowing when it would happen. Because of that, it managed to startle her every time. Poor Bones had peed in the house more than once, which was uncommon for him. At first, she'd tried to catch who was doing it so she could plead her case, but by the time she got outside, they were gone, the final vestiges of their fun just the smoke left behind and the scent of sulfur and whatever else was included in firecrackers.

Last night had been different, and now Emmanuelle was afraid to go outside at all, not just when the fireworks were going off. What she'd seen hadn't made sense, yet it hovered there in her mind. Rather than the image fading, it grew ever more vivid until she found herself studying it with her eyes closed to try and identify what she'd seen. The more she thought about it, the more the features made themselves known.

It had appeared in the lights, flickering along with them, different parts illuminated as if it were made of shiny, black mirrors.

At first, she'd thought it was the branches from a tree fooling her eyes, and she'd continued her march toward the men standing in the road. They hooted and hollered, running around each other, jumping up and down. It was like a street full of children, rather than full grown adults. Their faces appeared and disappeared as the fireworks leapt away from them, but it was never long enough to identify the culprits.

When a firework burst low over the street, shooting off frenetic red sparks, it revealed a face, torso, and reaching arms floating over the men. It was a matter of seconds, but the eyes caught Emmanuelle's attention. They were large and tapered at the outer edges, sparking red with the firework. And they were looking directly at her, seemingly black without the sparks.

The red firework continued for nearly a minute, sending the men scrambling for safety as offshoots came for them. Each flicker showed the figure in a different position, moving rapidly in her direction. The figure appeared to be the height of the large pine tree in her yard, which was at least fifteen feet tall, if not more. The torso was vast, the width of bottom branches of the pine. Its skin or carapace reflected the sparks like a dark mirror, though not as intently as the eyes, helping it to blend in.

Emmanuelle stopped and backed up several steps before turning to run back toward her front door.

The flashing red light outlined a giant shadow across her yard and porch, looming up behind her. Its arms grew closer, shortening the distance.

The red firework died off. The shadow disappeared.

It felt like her heart stopped at the same time as the light. Bones barked from the front window, the sound faint, his snout opening and shutting. He lunged at the window, struck it with both paws.

Emmanuelle was close to the porch. She pushed everything she had into her legs, urging them to get her to the door. In the fresh silence left in the wake of the firecracker, the only sounds she heard were her feet slapping the sidewalk, her own breaths, and the barking.

She turned her head to look over her shoulder, but saw nothing in the darkness. A porchlight across the street showed a faint yellow light, but no menacing figure. She slowed, turning her body back toward the street so she could squint into the limited light. There was nothing there. Planting her hands on her thighs, she sucked in breaths and tried to calm her heart. Bones still barked in the house, claws scrabbling at the glass. It wasn't like him to bark like this. He hadn't even barked at the revelers in the street. It didn't make sense.

Then there was a fizz, followed by a whistle, and this time the sparks were white, red, and blue, higher in the sky than the last one. The neighbors were at it again, hardly fazed by their near brush with the low, red sparks before. They ran back into the street.

But Emmanuelle had eyes only for the face that hung in the air a foot away, the eyes reflecting her own face back at her. This time she was only a few steps away from the door. She got inside, slamming it behind her, and pressed her back to it. Bones became even more frenzied, his saliva speckling the glass. Intermittent growls interrupted the barks, and he bared his teeth.

Emmanuelle locked the door, then moved to the window to close the curtains, afraid of what she might see through the panes of glass. She sunk into the easy chair on the side of the room farthest from the window and pulled her knees up to her chest. "Come on, Bones. Come here, sweet boy." Bones continued to bark until the fireworks died down. The tri-colored one had been their last hurrah for the night. Silence returned. Bones made his way over to her and sat down, pressing his shaking body against her legs once she lowered them.

Bones was a Doberman, sleek black, with brown marks on his chest, muzzle, and legs. He was not a small dog, weighing in at about 75 pounds at his last vet appointment. Emmanuelle kept him off the furniture, typically, but she coaxed him up onto her lap, and the two of them huddled in the chair that night, afraid to move.

Now, as they listened to the fireworks once more going off, Emmanuelle fought not to look outside. She didn't know what she would do if she saw it again. Not looking meant she didn't know if she'd been crazy or not. There could be nothing there, proving she'd imagined it all. After all, the men clearly hadn't seen anything.

It was so clear to her now. The large, black, reflective eyes. Long, sinuous arms, entwined with what looked like vines. Dark teeth that shimmered in a wide mouth that had gaped open in those seconds where they were face to face as if it might swallow her down whole. It didn't make sense that it was only visible in the light from fireworks, but that's how it had appeared. She didn't understand why it hadn't grabbed her when it had a chance. It had been so close to her in that final moment.

She'd only moved into this neighborhood about a month ago. Her old neighborhood had strict covenants enforced by an HOA, and fireworks had been forbidden. Surrounded by dry fields, the fear had been that one would catch fire, and people had been pretty good about following the rules. There had been an occasional bottle rocket or giggling children with sparklers in the street, who doused them in their wading pools when they became bored of trying to make complete shapes in the air with the bright white light. No full-on fireworks like these.

This neighborhood was different from her old one in many ways. Less friendly, for one. The old neighbors had baked each other goodies at the holidays, held neighborhood picnics on the Fourth of July, and kept up a neighborhood watch. Here, everyone eyed each other with suspicion. Men gathered in each other's garages to drink beer together and hold loud conversations. Women only spoke to each other in passing or at the playground while they sat and watched their toddlers play. Most of these houses were rentals, including Emmanuelle's. She was in a time of transition, having left her husband of eleven years, as well as her job. It had been time to stop letting people walk all over her. Yet here she was, surrounded by people who would rather stare at her as she walked to the mailbox and whisper about her instead of introducing themselves. People who were loud early in the morning and late at night, with no concern for their neighbors. People who revved their engines all day on Saturdays as they worked on cars and motorcycles in their driveways. People who set off fireworks in the street without a care for anyone or anything else. Bones couldn't be the only dog cowering inside every night. There were also veterans in several of the houses, one having even put out a sign asking people to consider those with PTSD.

This was a neighborhood full of people who had no interest in being kind or thoughtful or neighborly.

There were feral cats that came around looking for food and safety. Already, Emmanuelle had called in a local rescue to take away a mother and her five kittens, who appeared to have holed up in her backyard. She'd called the rescue for several older strays, too. Some of them were returned, their ears showing a small triangular cut that meant they'd been neutered and put back out on the street. It meant they were too feral to be found a home, and she was relieved that they hadn't been put down, but she worried about them here in a place where people seemed to care so little about them. She kept bowls of cat food and water outside, and had already started looking into how to build warming boxes for when the weather turned.

She'd felt safe in her old home, even when her husband, George, was away. There, it had felt like her neighbors would be there if anything happened. Here, she felt like it would be her neighbors who perpetrated whatever happened. They were shady, and at least one husband clearly abused his wife, who sped through her day, hardly leaving the house. Even then it seemed to be solely for the purpose of grocery shopping and running other quick errands.

Emmanuelle had tried relaxing on her front porch like she'd done in the old house, but that was when she'd found that the harsh voices of the men and the soiled looks they gave her were frightening. Instead, she moved to the back porch, and spent most of her time inside. Bones got walked twice a day to a nearby park with brown, crunchy grass and a small playground full of aged wood chips that wouldn't cushion a fall to save a life. They'd been tramped and tamped down over the years, and the city didn't seem to be replacing them or repairing the weathered swings and wood of the play structure. More often than not, a kid howled as she walked by, sporting a splinter or a cut from the jagged edges of the toys. With all the ferals around, the sandbox was a litter box, plain and simple, yet there were always children digging away and driving their toy dump trucks in it.

Everyone in this neighborhood looked tired and angry all the time, and it seemed to be exactly how they actually felt. They worked long hours and had only their rundown houses and rusting cars to show for it. Many of the houses needed paint jobs, fences were missing boards, and roofs had dark spots where tiles had been torn away. The windows were perpetually dirty, the porches sagging.

But it was home now, and she needed to adapt. With the new job, this was what she could afford. It seemed to be better than apartment living, but now she questioned how true that might be. It certainly wasn't any quieter than an apartment. Balls struck her house on the regular, causing her to jump. Music pumped out of more than one house on most nights, and the drunken parties went late into the night on weekends. Everything revolved around work and drinking. They were always doing one or the other.

None of that explained how she'd seen a creature of some sort illuminated by fireworks.

Something scraped against the window.

Emmanuelle placed a hand on Bones and kept still, holding her breath. She stared at the window.

The bursting lights outside created a flickering shadow against the curtains. A long arm, sharp claws.

Bones launched off the chair and ran to the couch that backed up to the window. He stuck his head through the curtains, barking and growling, his body tensed and coiled, tail tucked.

She stood up and moved behind him, willing herself to open the curtains and prove there was nothing there.

The shape moved, contorted, the shadow shrinking down as if it the thing had come closer still to the window.

It scraped the side of the house, sounding like a large branch, but there were no trees close enough to touch the building. Then there came a loud *thump*, a collision with the wall.

Bones shrunk back, still keeping his body between Emmanuelle and the window.

She reached out a hand that visibly shook, hovering it next to the curtains.

The shadow shifted, and she jerked her hand back.

No way she could open those curtains.

Emmanuelle decided to go up to the attic instead and use the small window to look down and see if there was anything in the lights of the fireworks going off right now. Chances are, it would prove she'd been imagining things, and she could return to simply being miserable about the barrage of light and explosions. Something else had hit the house. Maybe it was a firework. Maybe one of the men was screwing around in her yard.

She could keep telling herself that, but it wasn't making it any easier to open the curtains and look out.

She moved away from the couch and slapped her leg to get Bones' attention. He came to her side, sticking close, and they went to the spiral staircase in the corner of the living room that led up to the attic. She'd never seen a setup like this, and it had actually drawn her to the small ranch-style home. It felt quirky. The metal pinged as she walked up the narrow stairs, which were thinner on the interior than on the exterior due to being attached to a large metal pole in the center. Bones hesitated at the bottom, not fond of the strange metal stairs. He'd come from a large, multi-story home, where a divorcing couple decided it was better to find him a loving home than to try to decide which of them would get custody. Emmanuelle had been tempted to talk to them about the divorce, as she didn't have any friends who'd gone through one, but it had felt in poor taste, and she'd just nodded at their explanation and taken Bones home with her. He was accustomed to large, carpeted stairs. He did eventually follow once she got to the top, making his way up with quick bounds in order to arrive beside her once again, his large form protective and seeking protection at the same time.

The window was filthy. She didn't own a ladder to climb up outside to get the grime off. She wiped away at the interior glass and squinted through the dirt and dust of the circular window. At first, she saw only the dim glow of a lighter, fragmented around the dust. Then the flare of light as the wick caught fire. Darkness fell again, but only for a moment, and then the colorful sparks filled the air once more. For a brief moment, the joy and pleasure at seeing fireworks bloomed again in

Emmanuelle's chest, but that childish pleasure dissipated quickly, leaving stark terror behind.

Directly outside the window, a black eye coalesced. It shone at her, malice clear in its depths.

She stumbled back, away from the window.

Bones put himself in front of Emmanuelle and barked at the window.

The eye flickered in the light of the fireworks, there one second and gone the next.

During a bright pop of light, a hand shot toward the window, the fingers long and taloned. Glass shattered, spraying toward her in a painful shower, glinting with the colors of the fireworks, blue and green, followed by red and white.

The hand came through the window, arm stretching toward her, but as the body pressed against the house, it blocked the light.

The limb disappeared.

Emmanuelle turned and ran for the stairs. "Bones! Come."

She didn't know if the thing could still harm her if it was invisible, and she didn't intend to find out. The steps were tricky to maneuver quickly. She missed a step and stumbled forward, but caught herself on the railing. Her hands shook, as did her legs, and she forced herself to slow down.

Bones hovered at the top of the stairs, facing into the attic, and barking. He looked down at Emmanuelle then back to the attic.

"Come, Bones! Come!"

The barking became more frenzied as Emmanuelle reached the last few stairs. She looked up just as Bones raced back into the attic and out of sight.

Fearing her dog would get hurt, Emmanuelle called again, deepening her voice and putting as much command into it as she could. "Bones, come now."

Still barking, Bones came to the top of the stairs again. This time, he came down, looking back a couple times as he navigated the steps. He got to the bottom and pressed himself against Emmanuelle, staring up the stairs. He stopped barking.

Emmanuelle knelt and stroked his fur, trying to calm him. He shook, but let her pet him. "It's okay," she whispered. "We're okay." He woofed a couple times. Then he licked her face.

Now that it was quiet, Emmanuelle strained to hear, watching the top of the stairs for any sign of the creature. There was nothing. She wasn't sure what to do. She thought through her options. They could stay here, but away from the doors and windows. With no basement, she had nowhere else to go. They could go to the car in the garage and try to drive away. That might be the best bet.

She stood up, said, "Heel," and moved toward the garage door on the other side of the steps. Her keys hung on a hook inside the door, wallet resting in the basket on the small table nestled there. The garage was dark, not having any windows, and she took a moment to stop and breathe to try to bring her heart rate down.

Then Bones woofed and raced to the large door, launching into the barking again. He growled, a vicious sound she had never heard from him before. It raised the hairs on her body. The sounds of fireworks continued outside, pops and screeches, men yelling, whistles. She opened the passenger door and called Bones over. He looked back at her, so it was obvious he heard the command, but he fixated on the door. At what must be beyond it.

The conflicted feelings returned. Stay here or risk opening the garage door and driving out? The thing was larger than her car. It was almost larger than her house. Could she get out past it? It had breached her house, come into her sanctity. Now she planned on driving out into its place.

It hadn't come inside before. Why now?

And why hadn't anyone else seen it?

It could be that it wasn't real, but then Bones was seeing it, too, hearing it, so it had to be real.

Didn't it?

Bones lunged at the garage door, teeth bared.

The garage door dented inward, damaging a space about the size of a car tire. Bones intensified his barking.

The nonstop barking on top of the fear pushed her anxiety up. "Bones!" she yelled. "In!"

Bones whined, but left the door and jumped in. Emmanuelle closed the car door and climbed into the driver's seat. She started the engine and placed her finger on the garage door opener, but paused. She couldn't bring herself to open it.

The door bent in directly behind the car, this time further.

She pushed the opener button.

Hands clenched on the wheel, she stared intently into the rearview mirror as the door rolled up. It was agonizing in its slowness. Bones whined again, but didn't bark. He had hunched over, his ears low. His fear both amplified her own and brought out a certain protectiveness in her.

There were no fireworks. They'd paused, or perhaps even finished for the night. An unknown period of time had passed. Emmanuelle had no idea what time it was now.

The damaged parts of the door hit the top, freezing the bottom only about five feet from the ground. It clunked and jerked, then stilled again. The overhead light flickered.

Movement in the street told her the men were still out. More fireworks would follow. She put the car into reverse and backed out slowly, gauging the distance between the car and the stuck garage door. She couldn't tell if there was enough room. At the very least, it might be high enough that it would only scrape the car. She had to take the chance.

As the trunk reached the garage door, the fireworks began again.

A screaming stream of sparking light shot toward the garage, and the creature burst into visibility. It stood in the center of the driveway, legs spread, arms at its sides, as it if were waiting for her.

Emmanuelle stepped on the gas, reversing toward the creature.

It leaned downward, reaching for her.

A sharp *ping* in front of the car startled her, and she looked forward, afraid of what she might see. Was there another creature?

The antenna vibrated. It had hit the garage door, though her car had fit under it.

The car slammed to a stop. When she looked back, she'd hit the creature. It stood strong against the vehicle.

Her tires screeched and the car jerked. Something slammed down on the roof and scraped. Metal screamed.

She pressed the gas pedal down harder. The stench of hot rubber entered through the vents.

Three talons punctured the roof, one directly in front of her face. A frisson of warm energy came off it, a zap shooting the tip of her nose like static electricity, but more painful. The talon gleamed, black and glossy like the creature's eyes.

The talons cut through the roof like a knife through warm butter. A high-pitched screech came from each lengthening cut. Emmanuelle ducked to the right as the one closest to her came nearer.

Bones lunged, snapping his jaws around the talon and jerking his head, worrying at the claw until it tore lose. He whined as if it had hurt, dropping the talon on the floor. Sparking black blood dripped into her lap, sending electrical currents through her thigh. She screamed as the hot, sharp shocks coursed down her leg.

In the midst of her pain and fear, she realized this meant the creature could be hurt, at least when the fireworks were active.

The talons withdrew from the car.

Emmanuelle put the car in Drive, pulled forward a couple feet, then reversed, steering around the legs of the creature. In the street, she sent the men scattering as her car shot through them.

The creature raced after her, but as the lights of the last set of fireworks died off, it disappeared again.

Emmanuelle reached over to pet Bones. "We're staying at a hotel tonight, boy, and we're coming back with a plan." He licked her hand once. She knew he understood.

***

The next day, Emmanuelle pulled up in front of her driveway, finding the garage door still stuck open as she'd left it. In the backseat were items she'd bought at the store on the way back. She pulled into the garage and hit the button to close the door. It jerked at first, but then rolled down behind the car. She figured she wouldn't be going out that way again until she could get someone to fix it.

She took the bags inside, Bones darting ahead of her into the house. He ran around, sniffing at the furniture, the floor, the door, the windows, everything, as if checking to make sure it was safe. Shockingly, there were no signs that anyone had entered. This wasn't the type of neighborhood one would normally leave their doors open to all night without a visit from a criminal or even a curious neighbor. If anyone had come in, they hadn't disturbed or taken anything. A quick walkthrough confirmed it.

After having a quick breakfast, Emmanuelle started setting the house up for nightfall and the beginning of the fireworks. She unpacked everything, assembled some items, and went to work figuring out where to put them. The hotel hadn't been restful, but she'd gotten a lot done while there. Bones had curled up on the bed and slept most of the night. He, at least, had felt safer away from the house.

Hours of preparation passed before dusk hit. The house grew cooler, the light dimmer. Emmanuelle opened the curtains on the front window and settled into her chair, facing it. Bones sat by her feet, his eyes also intent on the window.

"This ends tonight, sweet boy, but it's going to be a rough night first." She petted him, his fur thick, but smooth against her hand. She'd make sure it was harder on her than on him. The preparations were in place, along with as many of the details as possible. It all depended upon the follow through and the creature's actions now.

The first whistle and pop sounded.

"Here we go, Bones."

He put a paw on her leg.

A cacophony of light and sound proceeded, as it had for what felt like countless nights. It was monotonous in its continuity, dull even. They'd set off the same types of fireworks repeatedly, and it struck her that their lives must be pretty sad if this was the distraction they needed. She made a deal with herself that if she lived through the night, she would think less harshly of her neighbors. At least put in a concerted effort. They were trying to get by like she was, yet she'd been considering herself above them in some way since she'd moved in. Because it had felt like she'd fallen in life, and if she'd fallen like this and ended up here, everyone else must have fallen to be here, too.

That simply wasn't true.

The lights reflected off a dark shape standing in the window.

The creature had arrived.

It stooped down to stare in, those haunting eyes fixed on her where she sat.

With a rake of its arm, the window shattered, glass raining down on the carpeting and the couch. It had learned from its experiences yesterday, and it stood to the side of the window, bending sideways to peer in.

Reaching an arm through the window, the creature kept its eyes on her, the hand creeping forward. The other hand came in and wrapped around the frame to steady it.

It stretched its arm toward her, the talon tips mere inches away.

A talon pushed the bit of rope Emmanuelle had set up, triggering the hatchet she'd rigged over the window. It slid down and sliced into the arm. The hand and forearm dropped to the floor, immediately disappearing. Black blood sprayed the carpeting, some of it striking her in the face and chest. It stank of ozone and sulfur, sending electrical zaps through her skin again. Luckily, the cloth of her shirt took part of the load.

The creature withdrew its arm without a sound. It didn't appear to be able to vocalize. With bright colors dancing across the surface of its skin, it slammed its body into her house in frenzied movements. Blood continued to pour from the severed limb.

Emmanuelle jumped up from the chair. She held a nail gun which she'd plugged into the wall beside the chair. Stepping closer to the window, she held it up before her and aimed. The first two nails went into the wall beside the window, but she adjusted her aim and stance, and tried again.

This time, the nails shot into the legs and torso of the thing beating at her house.

Instead of dropping to the ground as she'd hoped, it thrust its head inside and used its good hand to swipe at her. The talons swept through her chest and stomach, slicing into the skin. It burned and shocked her at the same time, the actual cut the least of her pains.

She called out and fell back, tripping over Bones, who had stood up behind her at the sound of his master's pain. He growled and leapt at the creature's throat.

It withdrew from the window, dragging Bones with it.

"Bones, no!" she called. It was too late, and she dropped the gun, racing to the window.

Bones had let go of its throat and stood, looking dazed and shaking his head.

Black blood poured from its throat, pattering on the grass. It wasn't ready to give up, though, and it kicked Bones before he could move, sending him flying into the side of the house just below where Emmanuelle peered out.

He whimpered, but got up and shook himself once again.

The foot came for him again, but Bones jumped through the window just in time, landing hard next to where Emmanuelle leaned. She took a second to check him over, but didn't feel anything significant wrong with him. "Go to your bed, Bones. Bed."

He went to his round bed near the entryway to the kitchen, but didn't lie down. Instead, he stood in front of it, following her command in the literal sense, though not in the way she'd meant.

An explosion of color caught her attention, and she threw herself off the sofa before the taloned hand came through the window. One talon scraped across her cheek and chin when she didn't move fast enough, but it wasn't deep like her earlier wounds, which even now seeped blood. It seemed like there should be more, but the scent of roasted meat told her the wounds may have been slightly cauterized by the energy coming off the creature.

Once more, the head and torso came in through the window, but it tore off a chunk of the wall over the window frame, increasing the space. It was narrower than the frame, so the light of the fireworks still managed to touch every part of it, keeping it visible and solid.

Next to the door stood her next weapon. She needed to take out its legs, and she'd felt she was more likely to be able to break bones over severing them. Grasping the thick, wooden handle, Emmanuelle lifted the sledgehammer and stepped through the door onto her small stoop. Its heft and her common sense told her she wouldn't be able to get many swings in before wielding it wore her down, so she knew she had to be exact and aggressive from the beginning.

With its head still in the window, she was able to march up to it and take careful aim for the knee area. Her initial swing was weaker than she'd intended, and she hit the lower leg instead of the knee. The hit wasn't strong enough to break bone, but it had to have hurt, because the creature reared up, slamming its back into the window frame before trying to pull itself out.

She raised the sledgehammer again, took a deep breath, then swung as she let the breath out. This time it connected with the joint, and a loud snap sounded, even over the constant noise of fireworks.

It fell to the damaged knee, the other leg bent at a ninety-degree angle. Grasping the bottom of the window frame, it tried to pull itself up, but fell again.

Emmanuelle raised the sledgehammer again, struggling against its weight. She brought it down on the creature's back.

It jerked backward, good arm shooting up in the air. Then it leaned forward, head low.

Sweat had broken out across Emmanuelle's skin. Breaths tore out of her chest. Straining against her own body, Emmanuelle tried to lift the sledgehammer again. Her arms refused at first.

The creature tried to get up. Its head rose, now too high for her to hit it there.

She thought about dropping the sledgehammer, but this was her last weapon. Pushing her will into her arms and back, she hefted it one more time, knowing this was it. One more swing, and she'd have to think of something else.

She adjusted her position, grunted, and swung, this time at its chest. It swung in a bit low, but it was still solid.

The creature fell forward toward the window, its head hitting the frame.

Bones was at the window now, barking and darting at the creature's face.

Emmanuelle stumbled inside and searched for the nail gun again. She removed the nail clip and inserted a new one. Bones' body blocked the creature's head, though it was visible behind him.

"Bones, bed!"

He didn't listen this time, intent on the monster.

"Bones! Heel! Heel!"

He came this time and stood in front of her, facing the creature.

Emmanuelle got as close to the window as the cord would allow, put the gun close to the creature's face, and shot the entire clip into it.

This time it fell.

She dropped the gun and pulled a tarp from behind the couch. Ignoring the remaining glass in the frame, she climbed into the window and dropped the tarp on the creature. Some of its body still stuck out, so she fell forward through the window, too tired and sore to try anything more graceful. Glass sliced through her pants, shredding her legs. She hit the ground harder than she'd intended and wheezed, the air knocked out of her.

Struggling to her feet, she pulled at the tarp until it covered the body in its entirety.

The tarp went flat. It had disappeared with the light no longer able to reach it.

Spent, Emmanuelle sunk to her knees.

Bones ran through the door and leaned against her, lending his strength. Emmanuelle pulled him close and watched the fireworks until they died away for the night.

"Next Fourth of July we stay in a hotel at the beach," she assured Bones, stroking his back. "Let the neighbors set off their fireworks without us."

The Blue Ticket

Picketers lined the sidewalk in front of the polling place. Red-faced and shouting, they waved their signs at those trying to get in to vote, not quite blocking movement, but certainly trying to dissuade it. Gina stepped off the sidewalk and took the long way around until she got to where the sidewalk branched out toward the elementary school where the polling place had been established. She avoided their eyes, but couldn't help seeing some of the signs.

Stop the Insanity: Don't Vote! read one.

Save Lives: Go Home, read another.

The Price is Too High, read one in all red.

The people calling for others not to vote were safe right now from the government's attacks. They lived the way the government thought was right, following the faulty religious principles that had been established. They were safe in their homes, safe from imprisonment, safe walking down the street, safe in interactions with the police. It was easy for them to stand there with their judgmental signs and call for change when they'd be going home to their secure houses and living life the way they were supposed to. According to the law and the translation of the scripture on which it was based.

Even Gina's own wife had told her not to go vote. "It's too risky," Layla had said.

"Yet if I don't vote, I have no excuse when everything stays the same."

"Your vote isn't going to overcome all the other votes going against it. Why put us through this every election?" Layla's voice broke.

"This is the only way to make the changes happen, Layla. Shy of a government takeover, there's no other way to effect change. I have to do this. For us, for the kids we'll eventually have. For our future." Gina's hands clenched into fists. "If everyone who says our votes don't change anything were to vote, it would happen."

"Don't lecture me, Gina."

Gina had opened her mouth to say more, but it never did any good. Every election year they went through this. Assaulted by ads for the candidates and misleading slogans, Layla always pulled into herself as the election grew closer. She didn't want to watch TV or read the news online. She didn't want to know how each issue turned out or even what the issues were. She wanted it all to magically disappear, and she hated that Gina persisted in going every single time.

The line wasn't as long as it had been last year. Fewer and fewer people were willing to take on the pressures of voting. As each one dropped out and accepted the apathy that kept them safe on election day, the risks became greater for those who did vote.

It only took five minutes for Gina to reach the doorway, which was propped open with a metal trashcan. A machine stood directly outside the door, a solid arm blocking her way inside. *Take one* flashed across the screen, the "O" flickering. *Scan ID here,* was next. She fished her ID out of her pocket and pressed it to the screen. A single ticket stuck out through a slot, sky blue, because it had been determined that blue was a calming color, especially that particular shade. She gazed at the ticket. Her number was 7834561. It would be easier if the tickets always started at one, which would allow a person to know what their chances were by how many had come before them. Of course, if someone were first in line, it wouldn't help them. Such a high number as this one made it seem that much less dangerous. This was probably part of the plan, an intentionality just like the color. The odds of this number being the one drawn felt slim.

The arm lifted straight up, a buzz sounding. Gina stepped through the doorway into the shade. She'd expected it to be cool inside, but instead the heat washed over her in a wave. It smelled of flop sweat and unclean bodies. She could sense the panic and fear in the air. It came in waves and infiltrated her senses, increasing her own trepidation.

The line continued to move forward. As each person stepped inside one of the cubicles, a door slid shut behind them. Red capital letters scrolled across the screen over the door, the words alternating between "Busy" and "Voting." Government workers stood outside each cubicle, their uniforms a soft gray, which had also been deemed a calming color. Personally, Gina found it dreary and felt like the color actually made her more tense. It felt institutional, like she was a prisoner forced to stand in line.

There were also guards. An entire army worth of them. They wore mint green uniforms, which helped minimize their appearance. Every color in the room, save for the red letters over each cubicle, had been purposeful to try to relax those waiting to vote. The guards stood with their hands behind their backs in a militaristic stance, feet spread apart and planted solidly upon the ground. There were no visible weapons, but everyone knew they had guns tucked at their backs, out of sight of the peasants waiting to vote. If anyone were to get out of line or stir up trouble, they would be killed without hesitation.

The man in front of Gina visibly trembled. Part of her wanted to set a hand on his back, between the shoulders, in an effort to soothe him, but there was no touching allowed. Even if there had been, she likely wouldn't have touched a stranger nor would he have necessarily wanted to. Her palm ached to offer that comfort, and she looked away so she didn't have to watch him struggling.

In opposition to the signs outside, there were signs and banners hung up all over the room. They read encouraging things like, *Every vote counts* and *Thank you for fulfilling your civic duty to vote.* There were pictures of happy people filling out ballots or holding them up to show off the dark marks that showed they'd voted. There were no guards in the pictures, no numbers or blue tickets.

One of the booths opened. A man exited, sweat running down his forehead so copiously that Gina could see it from a couple yards away. He rushed toward the exit on the other side of the room, disappearing back out into the sunlight, which flashed inside briefly.

The line moved forward once more.

A woman up ahead sobbed. It was one slash of sound, and she clapped her hand over her mouth, looking around in jerky movements. When no one moved or acknowledged her, her shoulders sunk down into a more relaxed posture. She wore a serving uniform for a local restaurant, a stain on the side of her shirt. It looked like ketchup, as if a dirty plate had pressed against her and smeared its signature across her ribs.

Someone else cleared their throat. They did it several times before coughing. The cough was so loud it made Gina jump.

Another few minutes and more booths opened up. The line moved quickly now as those in front of Gina filtered forward and stepped into their booths. As soon as a person's foot stepped out across the threshold, green letters flashed by on the displays reading, "Open for Voting. Step inside."

Gina thought about how voting had been when she was a kid. Her mom had always taken Gina with her. "You should always do your civic duty, Gina Marie. That's how freedom works." She'd taken it seriously when her mom said it, and she took it seriously now.

No one brought their children anymore.

Another booth emptied, and Gina found herself at the front of the line. The next booth opening up would be hers. Once she voted, there was no turning back. The moment she'd taken the ticket, she'd committed, but there was that part of her that thought maybe she could turn back now. She could hand over her ticket to one of the government workers and watch them slip it into a gray pocket, tell them she'd changed her mind. This was the point where she always started to doubt her decision to vote. She'd never seen anyone leave at this juncture. From outside, yes, before the ticket, but not after. She always wondered if they knew something she didn't. It kept her in line.

Gina's palms sweated and drops of perspiration rolled down

her back and soaked her underarms. She knew there was no leaving, no matter what the claims might be. It was time to vote, to do her civic duty and make her mom proud. While her mom was dead, Gina figured the woman watched over her daughter, keeping the same thing from happening to her. Her mom's last election had been a big one, one where a lot of changes were in the process of being made. It had also been Gina's first time getting to vote for herself. Busy at work until the last hour the polls were open, Gina had almost missed it. She hadn't been able to go with her mom, despite their plans to go together. Gina would forever regret not finishing up her work earlier and being there with her mom. It had been later that evening that her mom had met her demise, right there in front of the entire family. The first election where they extracted the price.

Gina shook it off and focused on running through the proposed laws she'd be voting on. She already knew how she wanted to vote on each one, having researched them ahead of time, but their wording on the ballots was sometimes so confusing that she struggled to remember which was which. It was stunning how many words they used to say so little. They were also carefully worded to try to get the result the government wanted. If someone voted wrong because they couldn't understand what the words on paper meant, it was better for those in power. Gina knew from watching what passed and what didn't how effective this was, wording it differently on the ballots than the information that was given out ahead of time.

A booth door slid open with a slight squeak as it moved along its track. The sign turned orange and stayed that way until the woman inside stepped out. The moment the last part of her body crossed the threshold, the letters turned green, beckoning Gina inside. The bright green felt threatening now. It felt like a warning. *Go, run,* it said.

Gina stepped through the doorway. The door slid closed and the lock engaged with a loud click. She was locked inside now until every bit of the ballot had been filled out. A sign on the wall over the ballot machine read, "Insert ticket to begin." There was a slot in the wall. Gina slid her ticket into the slot and watched it suck into the wall, her mouth going dry. If there'd been any wiggle room before, real or imagined, that was gone now. Vote or die in this booth. She'd heard stories of people who froze up and refused to vote once they got inside. They were packed away inside the ballot box and left on the back lot with no way to get out. Authorities did not intervene. Couldn't, in fact. The boxes were set to lock until the last item on the ballot had been pressed or until a specific key was inserted. There was one key for the entire nation, meaning it had to make its way around to anyone who reported a locked ballot box. Some lived until their release, while others had to wait too long without water.

Gina always feared, deep in the pit of her stomach, that there would be an error and the ballot box wouldn't open even after she'd completed her ballot. Technology malfunctioned all the time, why should the ballot cubicles be any different?

A compartment in the door slid open. A pad lit up, showing the image of a fingerprint. Gina placed her index finger on the pad and held her breath. The compartment closed around her finger, sealing it tight within the rubber gasket.

The needle was fast, a quick jab. She winced as it pierced the pad of her finger and slight suction was applied to soak up enough blood for identification purposes. Here was the second place things could go wrong. If the individual wasn't registered to vote or had already voted in this election, an injection would be the next step. Lethal injection.

Time passed, and the compartment didn't open. A display screen showed a circle forming clockwise, creeping along. Her heart pounded as she watched the circle, willing it to move faster so she could have her finger back. The pad absorbed her body heat and warmed her finger in return. A nerve in her cheek twitched just below her eye.

The circle completed, and still the compartment did not open.

The screen flashed red.

Gina jerked at her finger, sure the cold edge of a needle would pierce it any second.

The screen switched to green. The compartment opened.

Gina pulled her finger back and massaged it, closing her eyes and drawing in a deep breath. She'd been confirmed as a registered voter. Her ticket was now connected with her blood sample and fingerprint, which would automatically enter her address into the system along with her ballot, though they were assured by the government that the ballots were anonymous. She found it hard to believe.

There was no way to change that right now, so it didn't matter what she believed.

The ticket pushed back out of the slot. Gina put it into her pocket, careful not to drop it.

A screen lit up on the flat surface before her: "Proceed with your vote. Complete ballot in its entirety."

"Yeah, yeah," she mumbled. As if anyone could forget.

A paper ballot rolled up and a pen rose out of the counter. Gina moved down the ballot, doing her best to interpret which issue was listed. She clearly marked each item, ensuring that the mark filled the entire circle, but did not go outside it. Everything must be perfect.

She didn't know how much time had passed when she finished. Her feet were tired and her knees shook. She slid the compartment closed, which was supposed to reset the ballot, and dropped the pen in the provided receptacle. Turning, she faced the door and waited.

The door didn't open.

A red light reflected off the walls. When she looked back, she saw that the screen was flashing red letters. Drawing closer, she read, "Fill out final item."

She'd already dropped the pen. Panic fluttered through her chest.

Gina peered into the receptacle, but the pen wasn't visible. It appeared to have an opening on the bottom big enough for pens to go through. The pen was gone.

She tried to slide open the door over the ballot, but it stuck. She pulled at it repeatedly to no avail. She changed the position of her hands so that her palm pressed completely against the handle, and placed her other hand over it so she could push with both at the same time.

It didn't budget.

Desperate, she felt through her pockets, trying to find anything that might help her open the door. They were empty.

She'd come straight here on foot, leaving her things behind at home. There had been no reason to bring anything extraneous with her. In fact, it was frowned on, with car keys and identification being the only exceptions. If one had too much on their person, they might be turned away or arrested under suspicion of conspiracy to commit voter fraud. The wrong slip of paper or defense item could be seen as a threat or some sort of cheat.

She tried at the door again. Her hands slipped, slicked with sweat.

Hot tears filled her eyes, spilling over to run down her cheeks. Her breath poured out in rapid, panting puffs.

She slapped a palm down on the compartment door. Hit it again. Nothing.

Finally, she tried pushing it forward instead.

It clicked.

The door behind her slid open.

Gina let out a deep breath and exited the cubicle, eager to get out of the building and back home. She veered left toward the exit. Over the door, a digital sign scrolled in green: "Thank you for doing your part. Exit here."

The light blinded her when the door opened, and she stumbled to the side, letting the door close behind her. She blinked against the brightness until her eyes adjusted. Looking down, she saw she'd just barely missed a pile of vomit. Someone's nerves must have gotten the best of them as they exited.

Her walk home took only a few minutes. Inside, Layla had curled up in bed, the room dim, blanket pulled up to her chin. She was on her side in the fetal position. This wasn't uncommon, and Gina climbed into bed, spooning her from behind. She wrapped her arm over Layla's side and pulled her in close, nuzzling her neck.

"Now we wait," Layla whispered. Gina barely heard her.

"It will be fine," Gina whispered back. She closed her eyes and tried her best to relax. Layla smelled like cherry blossom shampoo. The familiar scent soothed Gina.

They spent the next two hours in bed, never changing position. Gina dozed off once, but didn't sleep for long. At exactly 7 PM, the television mounted on the wall turned on automatically.

Layla burrowed deeper under the covers, her head now covered.

Gina sat up to watch the news report. She pulled the ticket out of her pocket and held it tightly before her. A lovely young woman sat at a news desk, face serious. She held a single sheet of paper in front of her. Taking a breath, she launched into the report.

"All ballot offices have now closed and the lottery has commenced. Each polling location will have one ticket drawn randomly. There is no need to report in if your number is called. Authorities will arrive at your home within minutes. Please wait for their arrival and cooperate fully." She swallowed deeply, dry throat audibly clicking. "And thank you for doing your civic duty. Your patriotism will be remembered."

The bottom portion of the screen shifted, a scrolling message appearing: "Stay tuned for the lottery."

The woman continued. "For the Eastern Ridge polling place, the number is 4571035. Next is the Oak Gambol polling place. 8329017."

She continued in this way until arriving at the Auburn Elementary polling place where Gina had voted. "The number is 1...I apologize. My mistake. The number is 7834561."

Gina looked down at the sky blue ticket in her hand: 7834561.

A sob escaped her throat. She'd never really thought she would win the lottery.

Layla threw back the covers and sat up. "No." Her eyes searched Gina's. "Please say it's not you."

Gina felt light-headed. This couldn't be. She watched the scrolling numbers on the bottom, waiting until they got back to the Auburn Elementary one. The numbers matched.

"I told you not to vote. I told you no good could come from it." Tears poured down Layla's cheeks. Her nose ran, face getting blotchy.

Gina still thought she was beautiful. She reached for her wife and put her hands on either side of her face. "I love you."

"Don't do this. We can run. We can go right now before they

105

get here."

Gina shook her head. "You know they would find us. You would get punished with me. This way it's only me."

Deep sobs shook Layla's body. She threw herself into Gina's arms.

Gina pulled her close. They stayed this way until a knock sounded at the front door. Climbing out of bed, Gina said, "Stay in here. There's no reason for you to watch."

On the television screen, images flashed. Camera crews followed the election authorities, recording it as they approached a variety of front doors. Some lottery winners fought. Some ran, caught on cameras mounted on helicopters that hovered over the homes. Some came out willingly.

Gina looked back at her wife one more time, committing her face to memory. Then she closed the door, the sobs still coming through. Opening the front door, she held her chin high and stepped outside. The officials backed up, leaving space for her to step out onto the street with them. She turned her back to them and knelt on the ground, arms folded in her lap.

Every election had its price. She had done her civic duty, and this time her ticket had been drawn.

Behind her, the soft rasp of a service weapon safety being turned off sounded.

Gina closed her eyes.

The Pitter Patter of Tiny Feet

The sweet-rot scent of a street full of shattered pumpkins filled the night. Toilet paper drifted lazily from a tree with barren, reaching limbs. Only one jack-o-lantern sat unmolested, one home untouched by the teenage savages of Lawn Street. The widow's home crouched at the end of the street in all its creepy glory, backed up to the darkened, skeletal woods.

Leaves skittered on crispy feet, a herd of detritus heading toward the widow's home. Light shone through the windows in patches around the newspapers she'd taped against the glass, creating tendrils of brightness against the dark.

Inside, a warm fire glowed in the living room. As gloomy as the house was from outside, the interior was tidy, a once loving home. The widow—once and forever known as Mrs. Morris, though she'd always loved Violet as her first name—huddled in a stuffed, velvet armchair. Despite the fire and the soft throw wrapped around her shoulders, all she could feel was the cold. Goosebumps pinched her skin. The clack of her teeth chattering battled the pop of the burning wood.

Ever since her husband and son had died in the car accident, the house had been frigid. Though she filled her belly with hot teas and soups and wore the warmest clothes she could find, warmth never embraced her. She had nested here in her chair, the fire as perpetual company, because the farther she got from

107

the stove, the colder she became. It had reached her bones, the clammy air seeping through the layers of skin like missiles seeking a target.

A tooth had shattered from the constant chattering just the other day, sending an ache through her jaw that exhausted her. She wanted only to sleep, to forget about her loss and the cold in the air and the pain.

But they wouldn't let her.

Eyes drifting shut, Violet felt her thoughts growing murky and nebulous. Sounds faded. Her body relaxed, shivers pacing themselves farther apart.

The sound of the crash, a hollow, metallic *whoomp*, jolted her from the limbo of near sleep. As always, the sound of her son's screams followed. Her husband, panting, his seatbelt clicking uselessly as he tried to disengage, calling, "Hold on!"

The screams persisted, a constant litany of agony and terror.

She hadn't been in the accident, but she heard it every night. As soon as she started to drift away into blessed oblivion, the sounds came, wretched and torturous. Night after night, she relived an accident she hadn't been party to, an accident that had torn everything she held dear from her.

Violet covered her ears, praying now, something she hadn't done since she gave up religion in her teen years. Words slipped from her mouth in a rapid procession of beseeching, of pleading that this torment stop. It wasn't her fault they'd died. Why should she relive it constantly? The pain in their last moments was more than she could stand.

Tonight had brought her a brief reprieve, thanks to the children trick-or-treating outside, but now her grief rushed back in. It was the only thing stronger than the dread, this grief, a rending of her soul. It tore at her with vicious claws and sharpened teeth.

Outside, the quality of the wind changed. It lessened by degrees, the air pressure releasing. Violet's ears popped.

Then came the silence.

Just like every night.

It was as if a cocoon had formed around her house. No matter what was happening to the rest of the neighborhood, the weather ceased to exist over 3235 Lawn Street. Silence made it so she could hear their approach.

"The better to hear your footsteps, my loves," she whispered.

From the forest behind the house came the crunch of that first step. It sounded tentative, but that never lasted.

There was no need for her to check the doors and windows. She spent the entire day checking and re-checking them, ensuring they were locked. It didn't matter that no lock could keep them out if they truly wanted in. It didn't matter that part of her wanted to let them in, to rush to the door and greet them. To hold them in her arms one more time.

The crisp footfalls grew louder now, closer. There were two sets of footsteps, one more rapid than the other. One step was always louder than the others, as if more weight were being put on that foot.

Next came the sobs, the sniffles, of her sweet baby boy. Only six years old, Ollie had been such a good boy. He'd rarely cried, yet the sound struck her deep inside, so familiar that she never could have failed to recognize it. These were the tears of her child when he missed one of his parents, when he felt alone and abandoned. He'd always needed Violet more than her husband, Colin. Needed his mommy, who rarely left their home so she could better be there for him.

It hurt her heart to hear him crying, his staggering steps. The seatbelt had torn him nearly in two, twisted as it had been. The sharp edge had slid through his abdomen like butter, impaling itself in his intestines.

She wished she'd never heard the details. Who would have leaked such a thing? Why did the paper have to publish it? It felt demonic the way they'd gleefully related the sordid details.

Colin, legs crushed, had tried to get back to Ollie to save him. But when he'd changed positions to arch himself over the seat, it had set loose an internal chain reaction, delayed only by how he'd been positioned. The damage had been lurking, waiting for him to shift. They'd found his blood sprayed down his chin and across Ollie's face, dark against the child's pale skin, all the whiter for his own blood loss.

Colin had stretched an arm out, collapsed, his hand landing on Ollie's knee, where they would find Ollie's soft fingers wrapped around his father's thumb.

What no one other than Violet knew was that her baby's final word had been, "Mommy," choked out in a guttural caw. She knew because she heard that every night, too.

When the footsteps hit the back porch and slowly made their way up the three steps, Violet released the keening howl that had been working its way up her throat. She didn't want to deal with this again. It repeated every night, and every night she was too weak to do anything about it. To change what must always come next. She couldn't face this yet again, but she had no choice.

The footsteps worked their way across the porch. So much closer now. Only feet from where Violet sat.

From upstairs, the sound of different footsteps. Quick and light, they ran across the floor above Violet.

Outside, the steps were heavy. Both sets.

From the kitchen now, a heavier tread, though still lighter than those outside. The refrigerator door opened, with the curt suctioning of the seal being pulled apart, the whirr of the fan inside, a peep of light across the floor into the living room.

Violet couldn't see the refrigerator from her chair, but she knew the sounds all too well. Terror hammered at her chest.

The lighter steps reached the top of the stairs. After a pause, the coiled sound of a slinkie came. *Sproing, sproing.* Down the steps zipped the orange, plastic slinkie. It was painstakingly slow, time stretching as Violet watched its progress with wide eyes.

From the kitchen: "Honey, where's the beer?" The refrigerator closed with a tinkle of condiment bottles from the shelves in the door. The footsteps began again, approaching the living room.

The sound of tiny, bare feet pattered down the stairs.

Outside, the footsteps stopped at the door. The knob turned with a slight squeak.

The cold increased. Violet couldn't feel even a hint of the warmth from the stove. She squeezed her eyes shut, willed it all away.

In happier days, Violet would have been preparing Ollie for bed after the craziness of trick-or-treating. He was always so full of energy still, hyped up on sugar from the candy bars he'd enjoyed already. Every year, Violet swore she'd limit his candy intake better, and every year, she found it so hard to say no amidst the revelry and excitement of the day. Colin would *tsk* at her, but he was no better at it than she. Ollie asked for so little. Turning him down when he asked for another piece of candy seemed unfair.

The exterior door creaked open. The crying ceased.

There were now four sets of footsteps coming at her across the hardwood floor. A liquid plop joined the steps, one wet splash for every two short steps.

She squeezed her eyes tighter, fought to think of the happy times. Halloween was her favorite holiday, unlike both Colin and Ollie, who adored Christmas the most. She'd wipe the chocolate from her son's mouth and tell him to go brush his teeth. His feet would patter across the floorboards then up the steps. Running water would indicate he'd started his bedtime ritual. No bath on Halloween night. It would keep him up too late. Violet looked forward to her annual rewatch of "Halloween," and she couldn't watch it until Ollie went down for bed.

A giggle sounded from the direction of the stairs, the sweet sound of her baby's voice. It felt impossible to keep her eyes closed, as if they were being pried open from inside. She wanted to see him one more time, whole and perfect, but she knew he wasn't her baby anymore.

The scent of rotten meat reached her now. She choked on the stench, so thick it slathered itself across her tongue with the taste of spoiled pork.

She'd been overwhelmed with always being on, with always being mom and wife. All she'd asked was that Colin take him out for a daddy/son date. That they spend some time away from the house so Violet could get some cleaning done and maybe even get some quiet reading time. They'd all been excited for the change of pace. Colin hadn't had fast food in ages, not with Violet always fussing about feeding their son a healthy diet. He'd pumped Ollie up for their date, dressed in a vest and bowtie, then put on his own tie, all for a fast-food burger and some time at the park.

The footsteps surrounded her then went to silence. Only the

wet plop sounded now, a soft patter on the floor. The cold was merciless, an icy ache that swirled around her, inside her. Her stomach flopped, her soup and tea burning its way up her throat in an acidic eruption.

The photo the newspaper printed had shown the fast-food bag on the concrete outside the shattered vehicle where the door had been wrenched open by the emergency responders. The small toy car from the child's meal had rolled several feet, and the paper had placed a closeup of it, the real car a blur behind it, right next to the one of the open door. She'd focused on the toy, trying not to see the bodies of her loved ones in the first photo, her husband's staring face, hanging backward over the seat, her son's slumped figure, so tiny in the vast sea of the vehicle's back seat.

The editor had been fired for letting the photos through, the descriptions, but what good did that do her after the damage was already done?

Their bodies in the morgue had been cold, hard, and misshapen. Marble approximations. They hadn't seemed real, not like the two people she'd loved so much. Pale, waxy skin. No expression whatsoever. Empty shells. The stillness and silence had made it all the more exaggerated. The chemical scent of the sterile room had burned her nostrils and throat. She'd thought she'd want to touch them, to say goodbye, but the horror of their dead bodies lying before her had repulsed her, pushed her to flee the room, to not look back. These weren't her darlings. This hadn't happened. She wanted to take it all back, to make them a nice dinner, to gather around the television set. She didn't want to be in a morgue.

The house was so empty when she got home, but it had rarely been empty since then.

Upstairs, the water started running.

In the master bedroom, she heard the springs squeak as something rose from the bed.

Her blanket pulled back, and still she kept her eyes shut. It slid away, leaving her exposed.

Something cold and hard grasped her hand, peeled the clenched fingers back.

Violet held her breath. She whimpered.

Into her hand slid the toy car, its wheels rolling across her palm.

She'd only wanted a break. What she'd gotten instead was the constant company of ghosts and a nightly visit from her dead husband and child.

Upstairs, the water stopped, bare feet pit-patting down the steps.

Unable to resist any longer, she opened her eyes...

...and found herself utterly alone.

Story Notes

One for Sorrow – Oddly enough, with all the holidays that have to do with fertility (sooo many), this is the story that addresses it in any way. On a holiday that has nothing to do with fertility. I knew I didn't want to write about leprechauns (that's almost the only type of St. Patrick's Day horror I could find), and so much of what we celebrate in the U.S. has nothing to do with the original holiday. I have a thing about snakes, and one of the things that fascinated me as a kid was the tale of St. Patrick driving out the snakes (which, of course, is now thought to be about the pagans being chased out of Ireland, at least by some). There's also the nursery rhyme, One for Sorrow, which is about magpies (in some countries it appears to be about other birds, like crows). It's both light and dark, and I wanted to include it. Snakes freak me out, but I think they're fascinating. A snake inside me would definitely freak me out. Finally, there's something a little freaky about pregnancy, even when it's a human child, and so much can go wrong. A woman spends her pregnancy worried about the what-ifs. Thus the story.

April's Fool is May's Corpse – I went into this one wanting to write about a prank gone wrong. Combined with having heard stories of people getting kidnapped for fun or as a prank, and having evaded an attempted kidnapping when a man tried to first lure me into his car, then to physically grab me to drag me in (he missed and I ran into a stranger's house to get away), this became about a group of friends kidnapping their fifth friend to play a prank, and paying the ultimate price for their stupidity.

The Hunt – I could have done a killer Easter bunny, but like leprechauns they've been done to death. I thought an adult egg hunt might be fun. Every little once in a while, I'm reminded that the filthy rich, especially those for whom it runs in the family for generations, don't see the world the same way as the rest of us. What might they do for Easter if they wanted some entertainment? This story is one possibility.

Safe Inside – I don't have a lot to say about this one. I love the face on the front of the Ghoulidays' covers, and I thought an Arbor Day story about both killer trees and one old, protective tree would be interesting to write. Plus, so many people are freaked out by the woods, though I find them comforting. A true crime podcast I listen to tells its listeners to avoid the woods, because they're scary, but when you truly look at true crime it's suburbia that's dangerous and full of secrets. The woods are just the woods. Or are they?

Such a Good Sleeper – *Trigger Warning: If you have suffered pregnancy loss or the loss of an infant or child, you may want to skip this story, as it deals with the loss of a child.* I mentioned above that pregnancy is scary, and there are so many things that can go wrong. But infancy is also scary as a parent. Until a child is old enough to voice what's wrong with them, it's a guessing game as to why they're crying. When you have a baby, there are warnings like not putting bedding or bumpers in the crib, being sure to put the baby on its back, etc. Unfortunately, no matter how right you do everything, a child may still die from something like SIDS or an undiagnosed issue. It's absolutely terrifying. My son had severe GERD (reflux), and after waking up to find him not breathing because he had choked on his own spit up, I spent the rest of his infancy with him sleeping on my chest so I'd wake up if he stopped breathing. What if I hadn't woken up in time? That fear stuck with me, but there are so many fears related to parenting, and as far as I can tell, they never fully go away. They just mutate as the kids age and their situations change. Parenting is fear and guilt and confusion and troubleshooting, along with all the good that comes of creating humans. That's what this story is about.

Of Wicker and Mead – I wanted a little magic for Beltane. Though many holidays are pagan in origin, there are only a few that truly retain the original feel, and Beltane is one of them. It's about food and drink, fertility, the safety of farm animals, the green man, the fae, etc. There's fire, festivals, and even wicker men. I wanted to tie them all in together and show it from an outsider's point-of-view as they try to figure out what's going on.

Rocket's Red Glare – For all of these holidays, I researched the background of the holiday and nosed around until something inspired me with an idea. The Fourth of July gave me a bunch of interesting facts about the holiday, such as two of the signers dying on the 4th, several of the founding fathers believing it should have been celebrated on the 3rd, burning the king in effigy, and political parties celebrating the holiday separately, but none of these inspired me. Fireworks, though, are such a big part of the holiday, and living in the high desert, where we're often in drought, and having fled a forest fire encroaching on my neighborhood, neighborhood fireworks have become a thing to dread. I loved it when, as a child, our neighborhood in Maryland would gather and set off fireworks of our own. My dad had an old wooden cigar box where he kept some fireworks, and it would come out on the 4th. But it lost its charm when I spent days wondering if my house and all my belongings had burned down. I live by a park that still has the remnants of burned trees where the wildfire had managed to spread. Many of our wildfires are set off by thrown cigarettes or lightning or something small and simple, but the pines are dry and go up in flames so easily, the fire leaping from tree to tree. Point being, people setting off fireworks these days is a thing of dread. A monster only visible in the fireworks would make it even moreso.

The Blue Ticket – This one's probably pretty obvious, huh? American politics has become bewildering and frightening. Not that it was ever great. The more we try to take away people's voting rights, the better things get for those in power, so they're creative about taking those rights away. Eventually, what might they require for the privilege?

The Pitter Patter of Tiny Feet – Oh look, it's mom guilt again. I've been on online forum, read books, read articles, and spoken to other moms, and the judgment and misinformation spewed at moms is reprehensible. Moms spend a lot of time wondering if they're doing things right or simply telling themselves they aren't. We compare ourselves to other moms, and anything that happens becomes our burden. When something goes wrong, we internalize it and make it our fault. If everything isn't perfect, that's on us. That's what this story is about. I wanted to write about the creepy single lady at the end of the street whose secret isn't that she's evil, but that she's haunted by life.

Acknowledgements

One for Sorrow © 2023 Shannon Lawrence

April's Fool is May's Corpse © 2023 Shannon Lawrence

The Hunt © 2023 Shannon Lawrence

Safe Inside © 2023 Shannon Lawrence

Such a Good Sleeper © 2023 Shannon Lawrence

Of Wicker and Mead © 2023 Shannon Lawrence

Rocket's Red Glare © 2023 Shannon Lawrence

The Blue Ticket © 2023 Shannon Lawrence

The Pitter Patter of Tiny Feet © 2023 Shannon Lawrence

Other Books by Shannon Lawrence

Blue Sludge Blues & Other Abominations

Bruised Souls & Other Torments

Happy Ghoulidays

The Business of Short Stories: Writing, Submitting, Publishing, and Marketing

About the Author

A fan of all things fantastical and frightening, Shannon Lawrence writes primarily horror, mystery, and fantasy. Her stories can be found in several anthologies and magazines, and her collections and nonfiction book are available in stores. You can also find her as a co-host of the podcast "Mysteries, Monsters, & Mayhem." When she's not writing, she's hiking through the wilds of Colorado and photographing her magnificent surroundings where, coincidentally, there's always a place to hide a body or birth a monster.

Website: thewarriormuse.com

Facebook: www.facebook.com/thewarriormuse/

Twitter: @thewarriormuse

Instagram: https://www.instagram.com/thewarriormuse/

Amazon Author Page: https://www.amazon.com/Shannon-Lawrence

Goodreads: https://www.goodreads.com/shannondkl

Podcast Website: www.mysteriesmonstersmayhem.com

Podcast Facebook:
https://www.facebook.com/mysteriesmonstersandmayhem

www.ingramcontent.com/pod-product-compliance
Lightning Source LLC
Chambersburg PA
CBHW051232210726
48290CB00003B/921